FREMONT PUBLIC LIBRARY
3 3090 00629 8253

D1058394

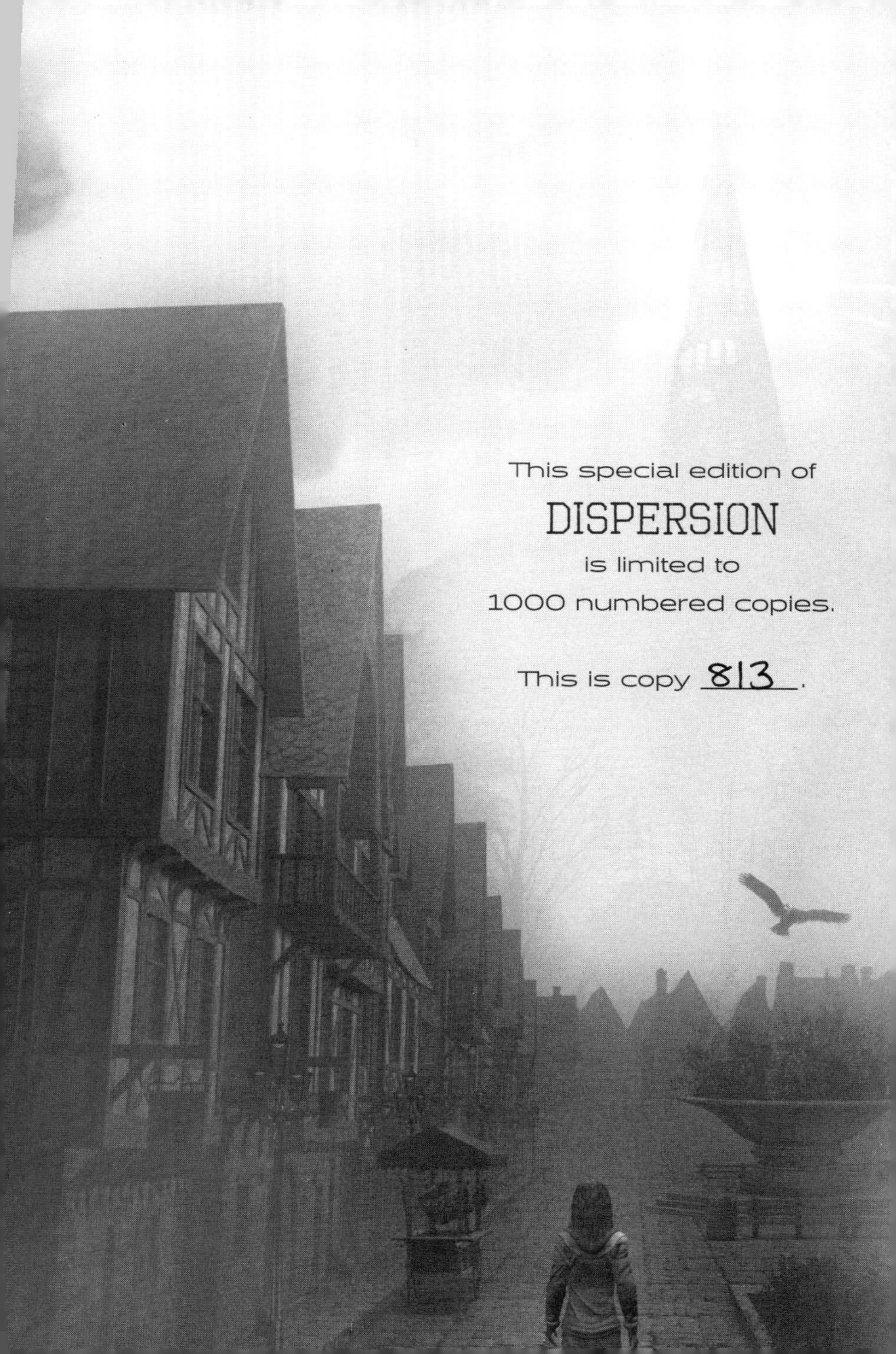
This special edition of
DISPERSION
is limited to
1000 numbered copies.
This is copy 813.

DISPERSION

DISPERSION

Greg Egan

Subterranean Press 2020

First Edition

ISBN
978-1-59606-989-3

Subterranean Press
PO Box 190106
Burton, MI 48519

subterraneanpress.com

Manufactured in the United States of America

1

It was late in the morning when Alice headed down into the valley of Myton. The air was still and the sky was bright; all she could hear, apart from the crunch of her footsteps and the clatter of dislodged scree, was the sound of damselflies and occasional birdsong. The cobbled streets and the courtyards of the slate-roofed buildings spread out below her appeared entirely deserted, and the gardens between them looked barren, save for a smattering of weeds.

As she drew closer, she changed her mind about the weeds: they looked more like cultivars, so their seeds had probably blown in from Ryther. When she reached the edge of the nearest garden, she squatted down to inspect the accidental emissaries from her home town. The garden's owners would surely have noticed them eventually and pulled them out, unless they were growing among near-identical Mytonian cousins. In any case, the plants themselves must have managed to negotiate their allocation of root space via the mutually-tangible soil.

She turned away from the garden just in time to see traces of dirt rising from the cobblestones behind her. The muffled sound that had alerted her had already grown inaudible, but when she bent down and put her ear to the road, she heard faint footfalls receding.

Alice proceeded warily toward the town center. When she thought of the crowds in Ryther on a morning like this, it was hard not to picture herself coming to grief among an equally boisterous throng that was oblivious to her presence. If the fear of being crushed or trampled was absurd, when she revised her mental imagery to portray what would actually happen as she blundered through the crowd, the thought of colocating with body after body was hardly more comforting. Mytonian flesh—for the moment, at least—had no power to suffocate her; the portion of the air she relied on would pass straight through any local citizen unwittingly sharing space with her windpipe. But the instinct telling her to turn and flee was not entirely irrational; if her ancestors had wandered into the domain of invisible, impalpable strangers, without knowing exactly when an unintended elbow through the sternum would change from an irrelevance to a mortal wound, it would have been the height of prudence to walk away.

After spying on Myton from the hilltops, on and off, for almost three months, she had convinced herself that the two neighbors still followed the same cycle as they had for centuries. The diminished contact between the towns should not have changed that; it had merely left her with fewer witnesses to attest to it. But if she couldn't erase the lingering doubt in her gut, better to focus on the genuine risks: a grimy footprint on unobscured ground; an inexplicable thud on the cobblestones. These were hazards well within her power to control; she could not be jostled unwillingly into a muddy patch on the road, or knocked off balance by a thoughtless passerby. If she trod lightly and watched her step, neither pretending that she had the street to herself nor dwelling too much on thoughts of mingled viscera, she ought to be able to pass unnoticed.

When she started seeing dust being kicked up around her, she welcomed the sight and strode on into the thick of it. The more the ground she crossed was disturbed by Mytonians, the less chance of anyone noticing her own trail.

As she moved deeper into the crowd, she spotted a small collection of stone coins bobbing along at hip-height in front of her. She swung around to check that no one else bearing currency was heading her way, but it seemed most people here conducted their daily commerce by other means. As she pivoted forward again, she froze; she'd just noticed a small stone in her shoe. How was she meant to deal with that? Any onlooker who saw it being shaken out would be in no doubt that they were watching an intruder—but if she kept walking and did nothing, she'd risk bringing the stone down on other people's feet, bearing a significant portion of her bodyweight. She'd once read a children's story in which a near-identical scenario led to all those whose toes were trodden on blaming each other, with much hilarity and well-deserved comeuppance ensuing, but it seemed unwise to rely on the same fairytale ending unfolding in real life.

Alice squatted down and slipped her foot out of the shoe, then felt inside and located the stone with her fingertip. She was about to try moving the shoe forward, while sliding the stone backward over the insole to keep it fixed relative to the road, when someone must have walked into her, and the stone ricocheted toward the heel. She quickly dislodged it and put her shoe back on, trying not to laugh as the familiar feeling of relief from disposing of the irritant became ten times more intense than usual.

When she reached the town square she was greeted by more floating coins, but also by a ghostly blue jacket, a pair of gray trousers, faint red shoes, and some items of pale underwear, all wandering quite independently of each other through the crowd. Not everyone could afford to buy new clothes as often as they wished, and these threadbare garments no doubt still offered enough warmth and modesty to be better than nothing. Alice had been scrupulous in her own preparations, but she took the sleeve of her jacket between her thumb and forefinger just to check, reassuring herself of the fabric's undiminished presence. Unless the tailors had cheated her egregiously, everything she was wearing had been picked, woven, cut and stitched in no more than ten or twelve days.

She stopped to survey the buildings around her. She'd heard esteemed painters argue that "true art" could only be made with pigments that had been refined down to the fraction that cycled along with the artist's own flesh, rendering the work visible to their fellow townsfolk for a year or two before slipping away—but thankfully the signage for most places of business was created by people of a more practical bent, and the restaurants and taverns of Myton announced themselves clearly, even to this unwelcome visitor. She strode from establishment to establishment, timidly at first, afraid to step inside, trying to reach a decision on the basis of whatever she could glimpse from the street. But then she gathered up her courage and quickly followed a patron through the swinging doors of Lydia's Alehouse.

The front room was packed with benches and long tables. Spread out across every stone tabletop were earthenware plates and mugs—and for an instant, all this unattended crockery looked like it might have been the aftermath of the previous night's dining. But it only took the first mug rising to banish that notion. Before long, Alice could picture at least a dozen of the more demonstrative customers, as they gestured with their drinks or prodded the air with their ceramic forks. The food was all invisible to her, which she supposed was a testament to its freshness, but every tipped mug spilled some watery portion that the drinker's mouth could not impede, briefly forming puddles that drained away through the channels carved into the floor.

She could not have wished for a busier venue, and she could only hope its popularity would persist long into the evening—to the point that no one would be able to keep track of all the customers coming and going.

The outhouse, as befitted a well-patronized tavern, had no less than four private stalls. Alice lingered unwillingly at the entrance for a while, afraid that if she staked her claim too early her protracted presence might be noticed. She'd be unable to hear enquiries about her health, let alone respond to them, and if a doctor was summoned and the door kicked in, the jig would be up. But if she dawdled here so long that she ended up half-visible, the first customer to spot that scatological wraith would have no trouble blocking her escape.

She retreated a few steps and stood beside the path that led from the tavern, so she could watch people come and go by the dust they raised. Once she was satisfied that she could read the traffic, correlating the arrivals and departures on the path with the unambiguous motion of the doors to the stalls, she waited until she was sure that no one would witness the signs of her own entry, and then she took her place in the fourth stall.

Standing beside the pit, she realized that she could still smell nothing of Myton; only the wind-borne traces of wild nature could interact with her olfactory organ here, so she might as well have been out walking on an unspoiled heath.

That pleasant state wouldn't last, but its gradual decline would be informative. Once she was fully aware of a stink appropriate to her surroundings, she'd know that she'd truly arrived in Myton, ready to see and be seen by her neighbors as an equal for the next three days.

2

As Alice walked away from the outhouse, she noticed a gap in the fence that led directly onto the street. She hesitated for a moment, but then declined to make use of the shortcut. The more she snuck about and shied away from the gaze of the townsfolk, the more likely she was to attract their suspicion.

She strode into the tavern as if she belonged there and weaved her way through the boisterous crowd of diners, marveling at how strange it was, not only to have gained the power to perceive everyone in the room, but to be firmly and safely deflected whenever she made inadvertent contact. No one was exactly deferential—the crowd did not part before her—but she was definitely not invisible either. People yielded to make way for her as best they could, given that it usually meant squeezing against someone else.

When she pushed her way out through the swinging doors she half expected a member of the staff to pursue her, if only to berate her for using the facilities without buying so much as a mug of beer. But if they'd noticed her at all, they were too busy to care.

She continued down the street, trying to keep her astonishment from showing even as she rejoiced in her success. Her first plan had been to find a neglected-looking toolshed to hide in, but she was glad she'd had second thoughts. It might have worked, or she might have ended up sharing a confined space with a metal scythe, just as blade and flesh began to vie for the right of occupancy.

The town center was well-lit, and Alice took her first real opportunity to examine the style of dress of the people she was hoping to blend in with. In the tavern, she'd been too overwhelmed—and from the hilltops, too far away—to glean any intelligence on the placement of buttons. But from what she could see around her now, the fashions of Myton had not so diverged from those of Ryther that she would look out of place; her shoes, her trousers, her waistcoat, her jacket all seemed entirely in keeping with the local versions of the same apparel.

Her confidence was bolstered—but there were limits. Even once she realized she was hopelessly lost, it took her a while before she could summon up the courage to ask for directions.

"Excuse me, can you tell me the way to Whippletree Street?" she asked a middle-aged couple strolling by, arm in arm.

"Back there, the way you've come," one of the women replied. "A few minutes' walk, then you'll find it on your left."

"Thank you." Alice had been prepared with all manner of excuses for her imperfect rendition of the local accent, but it seemed her mother's memories had remained faithful, and her patient coaching had paid off.

17 Whippletree Street was a terrace house, the last in a row of five. No lights were showing through the windows. Undeterred, Alice climbed the steps and knocked firmly on the front door. She listened for a response, then pounded more heavily. Every time she'd played out this scene in her mind, the door had opened immediately. But even if her quarry had changed address, the new resident ought to be able to redirect her.

She tried for a third time; she was sure that the coarse stone of the door was deadening the sound. Why wasn't there a proper door-knocker, or a bell?

The house remained dark and silent. Alice sat down on the steps. If she ended up needing a room for the night, how would she pay for it? She should have stolen some coins from the tavern when she'd had the chance—that would have felt less like thievery if she'd handed them back the very same evening in exchange for board.

She bent over and put her face in her hands. She really was the most amateur of secret agents; any decent spy would have come with a plan to cover this eventuality.

"You all right, miss?"

Alice looked up. A man had appeared at the door of number 16 and was peering down at her concernedly.

"I was looking for Mr Pemberthy," she said. "But perhaps this is an old address?"

"No, it's the right address. But he'll be at the meeting, won't he?"

The man seemed puzzled that this wasn't obvious to her, but Alice resisted the urge to slap her forehead and declare that the date had slipped her mind. Instead, she forced herself to make her ignorance plain; she wasn't going to remedy it any other way. "Can you tell me where?"

"In the meeting hall," the man replied, even more bemused now; where else would people meet, for an event like this?

"Thank you kindly." Alice rose to her feet and dusted off her trousers, then set off down the street. If she couldn't identify the meeting hall by architectural considerations alone, she should probably give up and go home.

DISPERSION

When she returned to the square, it only took her a few minutes to locate the building. She approached the entrance warily, but the doors were wide open, and a large and varied audience was seated on rows of chairs before a stage, suggesting a public gathering requiring neither invitation nor payment. She slipped inside and took a seat near the back of the hall.

There were three people standing at the front of the stage: two men and a woman, each with a lectern of their own. "We need to be patient," one of the men was saying. "No one ever promised that the benefits of this policy would come quickly."

"*Quickly?*" someone shouted from the audience. "Is that what you call ten years?" This garnered approving laughter for the interjector, and a few jeers directed at the stage.

"I understand your frustration," the speaker replied. "But we need to set those ten years against all of the preceding decades, in which barely a day passed when a visitor from one town or another wasn't walking among us. Even now, the detritus they shed might not have been entirely purged from our streets and our houses. This is not the time to conclude that our isolation has failed us."

The second man, who'd been growing visibly impatient, couldn't keep his objections to himself any longer. "Even if Mr Pemberthy is right, and our town is strewn with the dead skin of long-departed tourists, our bodies survive more serious incursions every day from hapless insects. *The air itself* contains all six fractions; every time we take a breath, half the molecules absorbed into our bloodstream will turn out to be useless to us in the long run! But nature has equipped us with ways to ensure that only those atoms belonging to our own fraction are incorporated into our flesh and bone. No part of this is new, or strange, or dangerous in any fashion. We need to end Mr Pemberthy's self-defeating nonsense, which has given us no benefit at all, before we lose the respect of every town in the land and our seclusion becomes irreversible."

"So we take your advice, and the Dispersion continues?" Mr Pemberthy replied.

"Whatever the cause of the Dispersion," his adversary countered, "it is *not* shaking hands with our neighbors now and then, as we've done without harm for as long as history records."

"History," the third speaker responded, "records no illness that compares with the Dispersion. And what Mr Watkins calls a lack of harm has actually entailed the slow erosion of our bodies' defenses. We've been lulled into complacency, and now we're paying the price. If we wish to be safe, we need to clear a much wider margin around Myton. Ryther must be emptied, along with Salton, Drayville and Bonnerton at the very least. Let them go live beside people who can see their faces every day of the year. And don't tell me that's an injustice, or a hardship! They'll gain the very same prize as we do: free ourselves from the Dispersion, and we free them all too, in the bargain."

Alice's skin crawled, but the people around her seemed divided in their reactions; a woman a few rows in front of her guffawed derisively, but others called out in approval. Her mother had been right in predicting that the isolation's tenth anniversary would prompt a reappraisal by the citizens of Myton, but only the gloomiest doomsayers had suggested that the proposed solutions might include this kind of escalation.

Mr Watkins waited for the audience to quieten. "Where is your evidence, Mrs Kenworth?"

"In my dead son's grave," she replied, with cold fury. "Or rather, in the portions of him we couldn't bury, because they parted from his body and vanished from sight."

"We all acknowledge the tragedy of this disease," Mr Watkins said, softening his demeanor in sympathy, but refusing to be sidetracked. "But where is your evidence that Ryther and Salton are to blame? After ten years of shunning them, to no avail, isn't it more likely that Mr Pemberthy's entire hypothesis is mistaken?"

Mr Pemberthy leaped to his own defense. "If a part of your body enters a state that is mortally dangerous to you, but entirely natural for your neighbors, what else could lure it into that folly but contact with those very same neighbors?"

Mr Watkins gripped the edge of his lectern in frustration. "And when your socks grow thin and your metal tools porous, is that Ryther's influence too?"

"Don't treat me like a child," Mr Pemberthy retorted. "We all know that fractionated matter disperses of its own accord."

"*Of its own accord!*" Mr Watkins seized on the admission gleefully. "It's not 'lured' away; this is a purely spontaneous process. But the only difference between animate and inanimate matter is that our bodies *labor* to replenish their constituents, allowing them to retain their integrity for far longer than any substance we refine and then neglect. If those efforts fail, then of course the result will be calamitous—but why point the finger at our cousins, who've lived beside us for hundreds of years? Who indeed have done much more than that, or they could hardly be our cousins, could they?"

The audience erupted into laughter, though Alice spotted a few people glowering disapprovingly at this ribaldry, and she could have sworn she saw Mr Pemberthy redden.

"Trace any lineage back far enough," Mrs Kenworth responded, "and we were all brute animals once. That's no reason to live like animals now."

DISPERSION

And on it went, with the three of them arguing their cases and conceding nothing to their opponents. Whenever Mr Watkins spoke, Alice felt a surge of hope; he made so much sense to her that it was hard to imagine anyone who listened to him remaining unpersuaded.

Eventually, a woman who'd been lurking in the wings came on stage to announce the end of the meeting. Alice rose along with everyone else, but as people started filing out of the hall, she stood peering toward the stage, trying to determine what the speakers would do next. Mr Watkins and Mrs Kenworth remained, talking with the remnants of the audience milling around them, but Mr Pemberthy had vanished.

Alice left the hall and retraced her steps, heading back toward Whippletree Street. A significant portion of the departing audience took the same route much of the way, and she had no hope of distinguishing anyone among them by the view from behind, but she quickened her pace to match the fastest walker in sight. It was late enough now that she could not expect the door to number 17 to open if she knocked, and she still had nowhere else to seek shelter.

She caught up with Mr Pemberthy as he was ascending the stairs to his home.

"Father!" she called out. Her voice sounded plaintive to her own ears, and she found herself unexpectedly struggling with her composure.

When he turned toward her, it was clear that he'd assumed the word was directed at someone else, and he was merely looking around to satisfy his curiosity. It was only once he realized that the two of them were alone on the street that the implication became unavoidable.

"Alice?" Her name seemed to have been summoned to his lips before he'd had time to inflect it with any particular emotion. No shock, no anger—but no welcome either.

As Alice approached, her father remained motionless. She'd been prepared to go as far as threatening blackmail if he rebuffed her, but now that they were actually facing each other, she knew it would only take a single harsh word from him to make her flee.

"You'd better come inside," he said. He turned and completed his ascent, then quickly unlocked the door and waited for her to join him.

3

Alice's father lit three lamps in the sitting room then ushered her in. The room was modestly furnished, with few ornaments or decorations. She hadn't expected to find keepsakes of his time with her mother prominently displayed, but nor did there seem to be any evidence of a successor.

"How old are you now?" he asked, as Alice took a seat. She assumed he was just making conversation, and was perfectly capable of performing the requisite arithmetic for himself, but she obliged him anyway.

"Twenty," she said. "If you didn't recognize me at first, I can't blame you. When I saw you on stage in the meeting hall, I wasn't sure that it was you until someone else named you."

"If you heard me speak," he said, not quite looking at her, "then you'll know why I couldn't continue with our visits. I tried to explain it to you at the time, but I don't think you were old enough to understand."

"I'm more than old enough now," she replied. "Which is why I've come here."

"To hear me out, now that you're equipped to do so?"

"To change your mind."

He met her gaze squarely now, and Alice thought she detected a hint of paternal pride at her display of self-confidence. "Have you been trained in natural philosophy?" he asked.

"I have."

"Well, that's an admirable beginning," he conceded, "but I've been studying this matter ever since the gravity of the problem first became apparent. I didn't reach my position lightly."

"So you're convinced that any congress between the towns is dangerous…" Alice spread her arms. "And yet here I am: neither sickly, nor some exotic hybrid who wanders lost between worlds. I am simply a Rytheran with a Mytonian father. My mother's body must have transcribed your contribution into her own fraction before it became inaccessible. So how can you treat contact as pathological, when it is clearly something for which our bodies are very well prepared?"

Her father seemed unable to decide if he should take offense at her speaking so freely. Another interlocutor might have been rebuked for intruding into his private affairs, but he could hardly insist that the facts of her own existence were none of her concern.

"Have you ever seen a victim of the Dispersion?" he asked.

"Dozens," Alice replied. "More to the point, I've studied their histories. None had any particular intimacy with people from other towns."

Her father shook his head. "I've never claimed that the cause could be reduced to a matter of individual contact; that's been happening for tens of thousands of years. What's changed is the sheer number of visitors moving back and forth, and the crowded living conditions at both ends of the journey. Half of every breath fools us, and once it ceases to interact with us it slips away. But if our bodies also contain other material from outside our fraction, and that reacts with the corresponding fraction in the air, what we shed will comprise, not merely pure gases, but particulate matter of ever increasing complexity."

"But as you say, it is shed."

"Shed, but not lost. The next time the same two fractions interact, some trace of the miasma that we and our fellow townsfolk exuded before will be trapped inside us again.

And our body will again treat it as its own, and advance it further down the path to which all such matter is directed: the repair of our own flesh. We are equipped to hold back the simplest impostors we might inhale or ingest—to test their enduring fidelity before wasting resources on them, let alone relying on them—but once visitors have seeded the air with more complex forgeries, we ourselves can embellish and re-embellish them, until our bodies make the fatal mistake of employing them for some critical purpose. It's as if a builder began repairing her house with bricks that turned to dust and blew away in a matter of days. A few might be used without catastrophic results, but in the end the only safe course is to ensure that there are no more lying about, waiting to cause havoc."

"Everything you've said has a certain air of plausibility to it," Alice conceded. "The story you've devised is not manifestly incoherent or illogical. But you or I, or anyone else who set their mind to it, could construct a dozen other accounts with just as much merit."

Mr Pemberthy bristled. "Really? And your own account of the Dispersion is…what?"

"My point," Alice replied, "is that all such accounts are premature. We don't yet know the cause of the Dispersion. My purpose here is to ask you to set aside your preconceptions, and join us in our efforts to discover the actual origins of the malady."

Her father's countenance darkened. "So my life's work is to be dismissed with a wave of the hand, by my own daughter? Do you have any idea how arrogant that sounds?"

Alice said, "I thought I showed humility, in confessing my ignorance of the true cause of the disease. But if your ideas were correct, even if the Dispersion need not have ended entirely in Myton by now, surely it would have grown less frequent?" She had no numbers with which to confront him, but from the tenor of the meeting she'd witnessed it was apparent that there had been no significant decline.

But her father wasn't interested in revisiting the debate. "I have a room where you can spend the night," he said coldly. "In the morning I'll find you a safe route out of town."

4

Alice lay on the bed in the guest room, staring up into the darkness. It might have been easier to accept her failure if her father had simply denounced her on the spot, summoning the constabulary to escort the defiler from their midst.

But he hadn't lost his wits entirely; his response to her presence had been measured and proportionate, according to his own reckoning. With decades' worth of Rytheran pollution still blowing around the alleys of Myton—when it wasn't gestating inside its unwitting accomplices—one foolish Rytheran girl who wandered in for a day would hardly be the difference between the end of the Dispersion and its resurgence.

She assumed that the meeting she'd witnessed had been called because the town would soon be voting on whether or not to continue with her father's policy, but since Mrs Kenworth had been given a platform for her views, they too must be under consideration. And, as absurd as her position seemed to an outsider, the failure of the current strategy might be construed either way: as proof that it was wrong-headed from the start, or as evidence that it had merely been too timid, and that much stronger measures were required.

Alice had barely slept when her father knocked on the door. She opened her eyes and judged the time to be just before dawn.

"There's a path we can take to the edge of town," he said, standing in the doorway. "If anyone inquires, we'll be embarking on a trip to gather botanical specimens from the slopes."

"And I'm your student, I suppose?" Alice asked.

"That would make sense." He hesitated. "Few people here would do you harm, if they knew the truth. But it's better to err on the side of caution."

Alice put her shoes on and followed him out of the room into the kitchen. "You didn't bring any food with you?" he asked.

"Three days isn't too long to fast."

He fetched a cup of water. "It rained overnight," he said. "I wish I had something filtered for you, but I wasn't prepared."

"Rainwater's fine." Whatever the precise mixture, it was unlikely to be entirely devoid of her own fraction. She leaned over the sink and gulped it down gratefully, picturing herself drooling even more than the drinkers in the tavern.

As they left the house, it was all she could do not to start weeping in frustration. If she'd been more tactful, perhaps she could have won her father over. But her own pride would not allow her to start belatedly pleading with him to reconsider.

The sky had just begun to grow light in the east. They had the street to themselves, for now.

"Is your mother well?" he asked.

"Yes," she lied.

"Do you have a step-father now?"

"No."

"I always cared about you both," her father insisted. "But even if you doubt the need for the towns to keep to themselves, no one can truly be part of a family when they're absent most of the time. I just wish your mother had found someone to make her happy, and given you brothers and sisters at least."

Alice said, "And I wish primordial life had taken its cue from the dirt, and found a way to use all six fractions at once. Wouldn't that have been something?"

Her father took her words as a sardonic rebuke, and gave up his attempts at conversation. They trudged down the road together, into the glare of the sunrise.

When they left the built-up center and began to encounter gardens brimming with vegetables, Alice recalled the scattered interlopers she'd seen on her way in, now hiding in plain sight among these leafy crowds. A farmer, working stooped over in the dirt, turned and greeted them, but made no demands for an account of their travel plans.

As they approached the edge of town, the path they were following came to an end, giving way to ground covered in patches of wild scrub. "I think you should be safe from here," her father said.

"I'm sure I will be." Alice stood with her eyes cast down. "If the vote goes your way, I'll never see you again, will I? And if it goes Mrs Kenworth's way—"

"Alice! *Nicholas!*"

Alice looked up. Her mother was approaching, stumbling down the slope, breathless but beaming. When she came within a few strides, she stopped to recuperate. "I can't believe you persuaded him so quickly!" she marveled.

"What are you doing here?" Alice demanded. It was entirely against the doctor's instructions for her mother to go scrambling around in the hills like this.

"I had to come and watch over you, if only from a distance," she replied. Her tone sounded like a plea for indulgence in the light of their astonishing victory. She turned to Alice's father. "Nicholas, I really am grateful," she declared. "I would have called on you myself, but these days I'm not exactly agile enough to go sneaking through hostile territory."

Alice didn't dare look at her father; she just waited for him to disabuse her mother of the false impression she'd formed.

"Rebecca, I never—" was all he managed before his voice faltered.

Rebecca strode forward and embraced him. "You did what you thought was right at the time. I understand that. But we can put it all behind us now."

As Alice turned toward him, her father began sobbing quietly. She looked away; it was unbearable. Any moment now, he would compose himself and explain what had actually happened.

"You're traveling light," her mother noted. "Never mind; we have everything prepared. All the equipment you'll need, and enough provisions to keep you fed for months."

"Rebecca—" Nicholas began again.

Alice stared at the ground, mortified.

"You've raised quite a daughter," he said. "She might not have changed my mind, but she did persuade me that I had a duty to see for myself exactly what you're doing there."

"All right." If her mother was disappointed to hear that he hadn't been entirely won over, she showed no sign of it. The architect of the isolation had agreed to travel to Ryther with them; that alone was far more than most of the townsfolk had thought they'd achieve.

As they set off up the hill, Alice caught her father's eye. He was not going to admit to anyone that, having been ambushed by his old flame, he had decided on the spot to oblige her—and Alice had no intention of embarrassing him with the truth.

"I told you he'd listen," she declared cheerily to her mother. "You always said the strongest tenet in his philosophy was to put the evidence above all else."

5

Alice insisted on helping her mother across the uneven ground. They walked with an arm around each other's shoulders, which also allowed them to speak in confidence while Nicholas strode ahead.

"Were you really going to stand there looking down on Myton for three whole days?" Alice scolded her.

"No! I just came to see if there was any kind of ruckus going on. If you'd been found out, I would have been able to tell."

"Really? Do you think they would have lit a bonfire for me in the town square?"

"Don't even joke about it," her mother replied.

Alice described what she'd heard at the meeting.

"No one's going to drive us out of our homes," her mother declared. "Whatever that woman believes, she won't have the whole town behind her."

The vote wouldn't need to be unanimous to pass, but Alice didn't quibble. As they approached the top of the hill, the Bonnerton Dam came into view to the north—a triumph of cooperative engineering almost a century old. If Myton ever did expel its neighbors and claim their land as its own, five sixths of the dam's water would end up going to waste. Could anyone take that prospect seriously?

"That's new, isn't it?" Nicholas asked. He was looking down on Ryther, but Alice wasn't sure what feature of the town he was referring to.

"You mean the sculpture?" Rebecca guessed.

Beside the road running eastward into town stood a sparse-looking assembly of metal bars, with the pieces Alice could currently see forming the edges of an irregular hexagonal pyramid. But the precise shape that any onlooker perceived would depend on both the fraction they belonged to and the day on which they were observing.

"Is it supposed to be some kind of metaphor?" Nicholas asked, with a tinge of disapproval. "Our mutual dependence, written in steel?"

"You'd have to ask the sculptor," Alice replied. "I think most people just enjoy the spectacle of watching it change without any of the pieces toppling over."

Rebecca said, "I would have liked to see a model of Mrs Neesham's proposal for the molecular structure of stone. But that might have proved too demanding." Alice considered that an understatement; she was far from convinced that Mrs Neesham, or anyone else, really understood how the six fractions stayed together in any unrefined mineral, when common sense dictated that if you picked up a stone, two thirds of it should fall right through your hand.

They made their way down to the road, but as they passed the sculpture Nicholas showed no further interest in it. Alice kept glancing his way and trying to ascertain his state of mind, but whatever regret he was feeling now for his impetuous decision, it was not as if he was burning any bridges. A brief trip to Ryther in order to learn more about the Dispersion need not come across as hypocritical or reckless—not to those of his supporters who actually understood his hypothesis.

"You have no checkpoints at all?" he asked, clearly uncomfortable to find himself strolling into town along the main road, with no authority in sight to demand an account of his origins and intentions.

"Why would we?" Rebecca was bemused. "Even if that could keep the Dispersion out, we already have scores of sufferers. But the afflicted themselves can barely walk; the farther someone's come, the less likely they are to be a source of contagion."

Rebecca led the way to the repurposed warehouse on a back street that she'd sweet-talked the owner into renting out for a pittance. The morning sunshine coming through the high windows gave the main workroom a cheery ambience, but the pungent smell of the reagents was less welcoming.

"How much did Alice tell you about the setup here?" Rebecca asked Nicholas.

"Not a lot," he replied.

"I suppose you need to see it with your own eyes to really grasp the details," she conceded. She gestured toward the hexagon of workbenches in the center of the room. "The hub is intended to facilitate communication and the exchange of materials, but everything in the wedge that lies outward from your bench here is your own territory, and no one should enter without your permission. Your accommodation can be reached from your workroom, or from the street entrance, and it includes a pantry and cooking facilities. None of which is meant to discourage you from going where you will in the town as the mood takes you, but given that the people of

Ryther won't offer very entertaining company on most days, my aim was to provide a self-contained abode where at least you could be comfortable."

Nicholas nodded. Apart from the fact that he hadn't yet agreed to any kind of protracted stay, it was probably now dawning on him that the floor plan implied the presence of more collaborators than he'd anticipated. He glanced down at the waist-high guard rails radiating out from the corners of the hexagon, then he searched the room until his eyes alighted on the clock, with a schedule of the interaction cycles spelled out below it.

Alice said, "Most of the time it really won't matter where you go, but if you're out of practice remembering the cycles, you might feel more at ease in your own section. We encourage everyone to wear stone pendants, and at least one bracelet or ring on each hand, but people can grow absent-minded." As she spoke, she realized that, while her mother has been suitably accoutered all along, she herself was still dressed for stealth.

Rebecca pointed out one of the benches, on the opposite side of the hexagon, where the glassware was all still sitting neatly in its racks. "That's yours. You can see the equipment we've provided, along with the all-important slate for passing messages to your fellow researchers." She paused for a moment, checking for any signs of activity, but it was still too early; her colleagues tended to be late workers, not early risers. "When you first take your place, just raise the slate with a brief introduction to let everyone know that you've arrived."

Alice said, "Let me show Mr Pemberthy to his room and get him settled. Since you spent half the night up in the hills, Mother, you really ought to go and rest for a while."

"All right."

She took her leave, then Alice led her father around to another entrance at the side of the building. "I know these all look much the same," she said. "But just remember that you're in number four."

"I haven't even brought a change of clothes," he lamented, as Alice followed him into the hallway.

"We can fix that easily enough, but you should probably visit the tailor today while he can still see you, and his scissors can cut the material."

"You have cloth from Myton?" her father asked, turning back to stare at her in amazement.

Alice laughed. "Not from Myton! But we remain on good terms with your co-fractionates in Haverfield." He still seemed puzzled, so she added, "We bought it mainly for filtering samples. So don't expect anything too fancy."

She showed him around his living quarters; after satisfactory answers to his first few questions, he stopped checking that every single item in sight really would keep serving him after the transition.

Alice led him through to the workroom. The shelves were stacked with vials that she'd filled and labeled herself, so whatever he enquired about, she could point to it easily.

"Everything refined here comes in all six fractions?" her father asked.

"Of course," Alice replied. "How else could we hope to study the Dispersion?"

"These aren't the methods I'm accustomed to," he admitted. "If I'm to collaborate, I'll need to be apprised in detail about all the work performed so far."

"I make copies of the researchers' notes," Alice explained, pointing to the row of hand-bound volumes on the bottom shelf. "It's up to each person what they choose to pass on, but most of the reports are fairly comprehensive."

"I see." Nicholas looked a little daunted at the sheer bulk of material he'd just committed himself to wading through. "Since you've read all this yourself, would you care to offer a summary?"

"Hmm." Alice's mind went blank for a moment; when she'd knocked on his door, she'd been fully prepared with what she'd thought was the perfect précis of the endeavor, but events had taken such a meandering path since then that she'd lost her thread.

"We've not succeeded in inducing the disease in mice," she admitted. "So our recent efforts have been concentrated on the samples we obtain from the afflicted, from the margins of their wounds. Our aim is to study the affected tissue continuously as the disease progresses, recording its fate whatever changes it undergoes."

"You could do that with researchers from just five fractions," her father replied. "All the material would still be visible to at least one of them."

"That's true, and we've done our best under the circumstances. But the protocols would be much simpler with your participation."

"You couldn't find someone from Haverfield?" he asked.

"We did approach a few people. But no one wanted to live so far from home."

"So, with the less elegant protocols you've been forced to adopt, where one observer is always doing double duty to fill the Mytonian gap…what have the results been so far?"

"Varied and confusing," Alice confessed. "Certainly, no one's expectations have been vindicated, but whether that's because no one's ideas have been correct, or because the method itself still requires more refinement, there is no consensus."

"I see." Her father frowned and shook his head, as if he'd stumbled on a group of incompetent students, but she suspected that he didn't view this news as entirely negative: if no one else's theory had emerged as a clear favorite, his own might yet prove more viable than any challenger.

"Perhaps we should make that visit to the tailor, before it's too late?" Alice suggested.

He hesitated, but he seemed more annoyed at being distracted from the subject at hand than by her presumption that he'd actually need the clothes. "Very well." As he followed her back toward the entrance, Alice allowed herself an unwitnessed, celebratory smile. Whatever her father's shortcomings, his work was the most important thing to him—and it was clear now that his work was here.

6

"How's the shoulder today?" Alice asked. Timothy had appeared remarkably untroubled as she crossed the ward, but he'd probably seen her coming and composed himself accordingly.

"Let's not talk about that," he said.

Alice nodded, chastened, and took a seat by his bed. She told him about her trip to Myton, playing up every comedic detail she could think of to make the tale as distracting as possible. He listened with a cheerfully attentive expression; when his jaw clenched and tears spilled from his eyes, she kept talking as if she hadn't noticed, and by the end of her account the spasm seemed to have passed.

"It must be strange to see your father again, after so long," he said.

"I didn't recognize him at first. But now that we've had a chance to talk, it's like stepping back ten years. He really hasn't changed at all."

Timothy managed a kind of snort of amusement. "Is that a good thing?"

"When I'm stubborn myself, I see it as a virtue," she replied. "So it's only fair to acknowledge that in others…it's something I can work with."

"Between the docile sheep and the mules you can steer, I'm surprised you face any difficulties at all."

"I baked something for you," she said, reaching down to fetch a small seasoned loaf from the basket she'd placed on the floor. "You said the bread was terrible here." She placed the loaf on the side table.

"Thank you. I could smell it from the moment you arrived, so if you'd forgotten about it that would have been torture." He hesitated. "Aren't you going to ask for something in return?"

Alice flushed. "It's not a trade. If you're willing for me to take another sample, say so. If you're not, that's up to you."

"I'm happy to trade," he said. "Not for the bread, though. I need someone to check my calculations."

"You know I'm not a mathematician."

"That's not important. What I've done is really not that complicated; it should make sense to any educated person."

Alice laughed. "I suspect there are ten times as many people who could follow the usual method of predicting the cycles than there are who could even grasp what you're talking about." Six linked clocks, in some kind of...abstract space with twelve dimensions? How had he even come up with such a notion?

Timothy said, "Unless I'm mistaken, the two approaches are identical. But mine can be written down with a few simple equations—not page after page of arbitrary instructions that people are expected to follow blindly just because they've worked in the past." He reached over and picked up a sheaf of paper from the table on the other side of the bed, where he'd had the roots soaking in a shallow tray.

"If you really want to entrust this to me, I'll do my best." Alice accepted the bundle of loose pages and placed it in her basket. "I'll put them in water as soon as I get home."

"All right then. I'm ready now."

She'd learned not to keep asking him if he was sure; the last thing he needed was her probing his resolve and prolonging the ordeal. She put on her gloves and unwrapped her instruments, then peeled the bandage away from his left shoulder.

The nurses kept the wound packed with gauze, and changed it regularly, but the packing was always loose by the time Alice saw it—not from any failure of care, but by the nature of the affliction. There was a layer of dark dried blood clinging to the wound, but even the small disturbance of shifting the bandage was enough to dislodge it along part of its length, and straw-colored fluid began seeping out through the gap.

Better to cut here, where she'd already disrupted things, than to spread the pain to another site. Alice took her scalpel, judged the depth by eye, and began the excision. Timothy remained perfectly still. It was as if he had a choice between flinching from the blade, or the exact opposite: making himself as unyielding as stone, even as the scalpel sliced into him.

Alice finished cutting, and caught the rough square of flesh in her sample jar. As she put the bandage back in place, Timothy started wailing, his teeth clenched now, a fist pressed to his forehead. *I'm sorry*, Alice thought, but she didn't indulge herself with any theatrical displays of anguish. If she'd wept along with him, it might have felt cathartic for her, but she knew full well by now that it wouldn't make him feel the slightest bit better.

She squeezed his good shoulder then walked away from the bed without a word. A few of the other patients called out insults to her, no doubt convinced that she did not have her victim's interests at heart, but she barely registered their words. If the six people on whose behalf she did her butchery could not find a way to save this man's life, she doubted that anyone else would.

7

Alice watched the slides she'd prepared being passed around the hexagon, with each researcher placing the specimen they'd just examined at the left edge of their bench and collecting the next one from the right. Mr Warren, Mrs Collard, Mr Grevell and Mr Pemberthy manifested as airborne rings and bracelets; apart from her mother, only Mrs Bambridge could be seen taking the protective box in her firm, fleshy fingers and extracting the glass rectangle to clip to the stage of her microscope.

There were twenty-four slides in all, twelve of them containing a thin strip of Timothy's flesh. The glass was of a kind that trapped every fraction, so whatever changes the Dispersion had wrought since the tissue was collected, the end products ought to have been retained—and unless they were comprised solely of colorless gases, they ought to be visible to at least some of the observers.

If Mr Pemberthy was right, Timothy's body had been polluted with material from various non-Rytheran fractions that had been incorporated into his flesh during the periods when they interacted with it, only to fall away a few days later. Though many different culprits might have played a role in the progression of his disease, when Alice had taken the sample it was Mytonian and Rytheran matter that had been indistinguishable; any other fraction should have departed from the wound long ago—or at least been present only inasmuch as it was present in any sample of the town's air. If Mytonian saboteurs had been trapped beneath the glass, her father ought to be able to observe them easily enough, undistracted by the Rytheran flesh that no longer lent them camouflage. Mrs Collard would share the same view. And while the bulk of the sample would still be visible to Alice's mother and Mrs Bambridge, to Mr Warren and Mr Grevell the same slides should appear empty.

In principle, the whole analysis seemed entirely straightforward. But Alice had grown wary of the risk that the people peering down their microscope barrels would be all too cognisant of the predictions that followed from their own beloved theories. How was she to keep them from squinting a little too hard and seeing only what they expected to see? That question had troubled her for months, but after her father's arrival it had seemed more acute than ever. She would never accuse any of the researchers of deliberate dishonesty, but deceiving oneself was far less troubling to the conscience than an outright lie.

"That poor boy," her mother remarked, scribbling her observations in her notebook without lifting her eye from the microscope. "You took almost twice as much from him this time!"

"I think I had the scalpel in too deep from the start," Alice replied. "But once I'd begun cutting, it seemed kinder to keep going than to try to correct it."

Her mother didn't reply. Alice wasn't sure if she was taken aback by this explanation, or if she'd started to notice a disparity between some of the samples that went beyond the usual variation. But whatever her suspicions, her task right now was simply to record what she could see on each slide. All interpretations were to be deferred until the observations were collated.

"You should go home and rest," her mother suggested. "It will take us a while to get through the whole set."

"No, I'll wait." Alice wasn't sure what she thought would happen if she left, but she was reluctant to give up the chance to watch over as much of the proceedings as she could. The sight of the samples moving from bench to bench reminded her of the time her father and a few of his friends had stayed on in Ryther for an extra day, and for a lark they'd organized a relay race between two teams comprised of equal numbers from each town. Everyone had had to hand the baton to an unseen successor, who watched for the approaching stick and tried to grab it—sometimes needing to chase down the holder if they misjudged the timing or the degree of steadiness required. Alice could no longer recall which team had won, but she had ended up rolling on the grass afterward, laughing with delight and astonishment at the whole glorious spectacle. A few months later, her father had told her: it's not safe, I can't keep coming here, I might be spreading a terrible disease.

Her leg was still throbbing where she'd cut it, but she stared down the pain. This wound would heal; it was the ones that kept growing that deserved her attention.

When the last of the slides had finished its circuit, the researchers closed their notebooks and passed them around to Rebecca's bench for Alice to collect.

"Take your time," her mother told her. "And if anyone's remarks are ambiguous, or illegible, don't be shy about asking for clarification."

"I won't."

DISPERSION

Alone in her workroom, Alice set about tabulating the notes. Unsurprisingly, the four observers currently blind to all things Rytheran had reported slides that were either sparsely occupied or entirely empty. Alice had shuffled in the decoys at random, but she'd kept a record of the slide numbers, and it was gratifying to see that her own dead tissue had not yet dispersed to the point of wider visibility.

Timothy's samples had received very different reports from some of the observers—but not from the pair who had been predicted to do so. Mr Pemberthy and Mrs Collard had been unable to discern anything on Timothy's slides that they had not also found on Alice's: a smattering of Mytonian and Drayvillean dust. Maybe nothing but their own shed skin, their own eyelashes. If Mr Pemberthy had been hoping that these traces of foreign matter were signs of victory, he was going to be severely disappointed.

It was Mr Warren and Mr Grevell who had observed features in the diseased samples that were absent from the healthy ones. At the margins of Timothy's Rytheran flesh—as sketched against the grid lines of the slide cover by Alice's mother and Mrs Bambridge—they had both noted a narrow speckled region, invisible to everyone else.

Alice was perplexed, but she was doubly glad now of her own contributions to the samples; not only did they show that any minor pollution from Myton and Drayville had nothing to do with the disease, they made it a thousand times more fanciful to suppose that Mr Warren and Mr Grevell had conspired to produce their results. Even if they'd sat down together and agreed on some sequence of invented images to draw, how could they have known not to draw them in precisely those cases when they were actually looking at her uninfected flesh?

If there was no deceit here, though, the truth was far stranger than anyone had posited. Mr Warren and Mr Grevell were from Salton and Ridgewood; regardless of how much detritus from either fraction might have snuck into Timothy's body in an earlier cycle, no significant trace of it should have remained by the time she'd taken her cut.

Alice rechecked all the notes a dozen times before concluding that her summary was accurate and complete. The facts would have to speak for themselves; she had no interpretation to offer.

She leaned back in her chair, wishing she had a further task to distract her from her wound. The pile of papers Timothy had given her still sat, well-watered but unread, at the side of her desk; she was sure they'd just vex and confuse her as much as the reports she'd just dealt with, but she'd promised him that she'd try her best to understand his ideas.

She picked up the first sheet and started reading.

8

"You can probably smell the bread already, but I'll spare you any need to guess what else I've brought: your papers, with some questions, and some papers of my own to show you. No scalpel at all this time."

Timothy was speechless for a moment. Alice took out the loaf and placed it on the table. "Three good things in one day," he said finally. "I hardly know what to make of that."

Alice handed him his notes. "I could follow the trigonometry and algebra well enough," she said, "at least on the level of applying all the rote manipulations I was taught in school. But to really understand what you're saying here, I needed to paraphrase it to myself, and I want to be sure that my interpretation does the mathematics justice."

Timothy rearranged himself on his bed. "All right. Paraphrase away."

"I think you're saying that everything about the cycles can be understood in terms of something akin to shadows," she began. "An inclined stick casts a shadow on the ground at noon, or a wall at dusk, that discards the details of its orientation in some directions, while preserving it in those of the surface upon which the shadow is cast." She hesitated, already unsure if she was making a fool of herself.

"Go on," Timothy insisted. "If I start to disagree, I'll make my objections known, but so far you've said nothing I take issue with."

Alice continued. "The cycles happen in a space with twelve dimensions, though the dimensions seem to come in pairs that are intimately linked, and also pairs of pairs. Each fraction is like an inclined stick whose direction keeps changing, following one rule of shadows: in each of six pairs of directions, the shadow it casts must turn in a perfect circle at a fixed rate—and a different rate for each of those pairs. So whatever town we're from, we all cast six shadows into the same six planes, and they all turn at the particular rate befitting the plane in question. Every fraction obeys identical laws; the difference between us lies solely in the directions we started from."

Timothy smiled. "That's exactly right. We're all weaving around the twelve-space in a very elaborate dance, but because we weren't treading on each other's toes when the music started, the rules we all obey, together, continue to keep us from colliding."

"And yet," Alice replied, "sometimes we do tread on each other's toes."

"You mean, we feel each other's presence in ordinary space?"

"Yes."

"Go on," Timothy encouraged her.

"Again, it's a rule of shadows," she said. "But this time, the twelve-space is carved up differently. Instead of the six pairs of directions that control the way each fraction changes, there are three pairs of pairs—and not even pairs of the original twelve directions. The whole framework now is askew from the first."

Timothy nodded in affirmation; she hadn't misunderstood the table of numbers he'd given that expressed the transformation between the two sets of directions.

Alice pressed on. "But it's these three pairs of pairs that govern the interaction: we can only see and touch each other if we both happen to have long shadows within the same space of four dimensions. Since you and I belong to the same fraction, that's always true for us—our shadows are always identical. But for people from different towns, it's all down to the way the six shadows that turn like clocks move their three shadows of the other kind in and out of different… I don't know what to call those three spaces, without spelling out their entire description every time I mention them."

"Interaction regions," Timothy suggested.

"I never thought of the fractions as being in motion at all," Alice confessed. "I thought the interaction between them grew weaker and stronger in some complicated fashion, but that was just the way it was. But in your account, it's as if there are three 'places' the fractions can 'visit,' and if any two of us are in the same place at once, it's only to be expected that we see our fellow visitor to that site, and not those who are in the other two locations."

"That might be stretching the meaning of 'expected'," Timothy replied. "But I'm gratified that it makes sense to you."

"I do still have some questions," Alice said.

Timothy spread his hands. "I'm at your service."

"Where is stone in all this, if it's not an agglomeration of every fraction? That's the popular belief, but it never seemed intelligible to me."

"I think stone is an agglomeration of pieces that each cast their individual shadows in only one of the pairs of directions that form the clocks. So they each go around in circles in a very simple fashion, without mixing up different rates of motion the way the fractions do. But those directions all cast roughly equal-length shadows in all three interaction regions—so stone treats them all even-handedly, without belonging to any of them."

Alice closed her eyes and tried to picture it; it was a bit like the diagonal that crossed a cubical room from top to bottom between two farthest corners, which would cast a shadow of equal size on any side of the cube. "So whichever fraction we belong to, wherever we go, stone is already there waiting for us, neither more nor less than at any other time."

"My calculations say it should vary a little," Timothy clarified, "though it might be difficult to measure the change."

Alice glanced around the ward, wondering if anyone else was listening in to this glorious madness, but all of the other patients appeared lost in their own thoughts and problems.

"Did you have any other questions?" Timothy asked.

"Yes. But that brings me to my own papers." Alice reached into her basket and took out a copy of the notes she'd made, summarizing the group's observations. "After a few days, the samples from your wound contained material that was only visible to people from Salton and Ridgewood." She handed him the report, bringing his attention to the relevant table.

"But if it was from either of those fractions, how could it have been clinging to your body when I took it?"

Timothy frowned, but he said nothing to suggest that he doubted the results. "Maybe we can map it," he declared. "If it stays intact long enough, and doesn't leak away."

"Map what?"

"You're going to keep observing the samples, aren't you?"

"Yes, of course."

"Good." He winced suddenly; their heady conversation had been distracting him, but his wound seemed to have reasserted its presence.

Alice said, "We'll keep watching, but what is it that you want us to map?"

Timothy stared at the space beside her, waiting for the pain to lessen. Then he said, "I think you must have found a new fraction, an interloper in the dance between the six. But one sighting won't tell us much about it. You need to keep following it, and note the times it appears beside each couple in the dance. Then we might finally learn something. Then we might find a way to chase it down."

9

Alice cooked her mother her favorite meal: potato pie with stewed leeks and pumpkin soup.

"I have some things to tell you," she said, when she'd cleared away the dishes.

"I thought you might." Rebecca sighed. "Well, get on with it, while I'm still stupefied by my satiety."

Alice started with the extra samples she'd introduced into the study.

"That was ingenious," her mother conceded. "We should probably start doing it as a matter of course; we can't keep the fact of it a secret, but we can still keep the particular nature of each sample hidden from the observers. I wish you'd taken the uninfected samples from someone else, though; no one should be carving up their own flesh."

Alice was inclined to agree, but she had no idea who else she could possibly expect to volunteer.

"I spoke to Timothy about the results," she said. Unlike her improvised tissue donations, that crime had been explicitly forbidden; Rebecca didn't want patients having their hopes raised and dashed by every tentative discovery. "But I owed him that, and it was a fruitful exchange. Because he has some very pertinent ideas on the subject."

As her mother listened to Alice's version of the theory, her expression changed from wary, to quizzical, to openly disdainful.

"It sounds an awful lot like planetary epicycles," Rebecca opined.

Alice was annoyed. "Perhaps it does, superficially—but unless you have an improvement to offer as elegant as heliocentric orbits, it's the old account of the cycles that seems quaint and ad hoc to me, not this one."

"Don't you think it's just the product of a young man reaching for hope? He's seen people dying of the Dispersion for years, and now the only way he can face his situation is to convince himself that he has personally discovered all the answers no one else could find."

"No, I don't think that at all," Alice replied heatedly. "His situation might well have focused his mind, but…

whatever physical processes underlie the cycles, he seems to have summed up the laws behind them more concisely than anyone else has been able to."

"Perhaps. If his formulas agree with the traditional calendric algorithms, you could say he's modernized the old notation. It's just book-keeping, really, but that's not without value."

Alice fought to calm herself; she didn't need to convince her mother that Timothy was right. She just needed to persuade her not to abandon any line of inquiry that would help to test his ideas.

"We will keep watching his slides, though? For at least another week?" Alice had not been included in all of the discussions that followed the anomalous result, but she'd seen the words "obvious contaminant!" on one chalkboard. After all her efforts to prevent the investigation from succumbing to anyone's biases, if they were going to throw out every sample that upset their preconceptions, she'd be sorely tempted to start wielding her scalpel in entirely new directions.

"We'll keep watching them," her mother replied. "I honestly don't know what's happened there, but it's not yet clear that we can blame it on the preparation of the slides, so it would be premature to discard them immediately."

Alice bit her tongue; she had what she needed.

Almost.

"They'll be voting in Myton next week," she said. "Do you think you could talk to Mr Pemberthy about a quick trip back...to amend his public stance?"

Her mother was amused. "What makes you think he'd take instructions from me?"

"He still cares about you. That's obvious."

Rebecca didn't reply. Alice couldn't see why the prospect of putting the request to him would make her uncomfortable. "If the vote goes to Mrs Kenworth—"

"Oh, people aren't that foolish!" her mother interjected.

"And continuing the isolation wouldn't be bad enough?"

"The isolation is a terrible policy, but if we find a cure for the Dispersion it'll be overturned in no time." Her mother rose from her seat. "That was a wonderful meal." She leaned down and kissed Alice on the forehead. "I'm heading off to bed now."

10

"You've seen enough to decide the question, surely?" Alice wrote on her slate.

Her father's chalk hovered for a moment, then responded. "I need one more round of observations."

"Why?" Alice scrawled quickly, then she paused to wipe a clear space to continue. "The vote is in less than a week!"

"Better to go back with a definite verdict, than merely raising doubts," her father wrote.

Alice was grateful that he couldn't see the exasperation on her face. What was this, if not cowardice and dishonesty—or at the very least a pernicious form of indecisiveness? But she'd almost lost him back in Myton with her blunt assessment of his work; she wasn't going to start haranguing him now, when she was less equipped than ever to judge the point where she'd overstepped the mark and was merely making him more stubborn and defensive.

She picked up the chalk again and wrote calmly, "Are you sure there will be time to spread the word?"

"Yes," he wrote, without hesitation.

"What about Mrs Kenworth's supporters?" Alice countered. "How amenable to your testimony will they be?"

He paused, then scuffed the slate clean and wrote, "They won't be swayed, but there are not enough of them to decide the outcome."

Alice wasn't satisfied, but she was at a loss to see what more she could do.

"One more round?" she wrote. "And then you'll take the news to Myton, whatever the verdict?"

"Yes," he replied.

11

Alice renumbered all the slides with her own secret key before taking them back to the hexagon; that way, the previous notes people had made would be no guide as to what they could expect to see this time. She'd stopped feeling guilty about her unwillingness to simply trust the investigators; any strategy that made the observations more reliable, or any bias more visible, was worth trying.

It was Mr Warren whom Alice could see now, along with her mother, but even with the rest of the participants reduced to their gesticulating jewelry, she found herself picturing them all moving through a vast, dark ballroom, a separate spotlight illuminating each pair, while dazzling their eyes so they couldn't look out across the gloom and catch a glimpse of the others. Her father was dancing with Mrs Bambridge, and Mr Grevell was waltzing with Mrs Collard. The fanciful imagery didn't really capture the grandeur of Timothy's scheme, but he was the one who'd introduced this metaphor, and Alice was more than willing to accept it as a substitute that mere mortals, unaccustomed to twelve-dimensional thinking, could hold in their mind's eye.

"You haven't thrown in some samples from a stray cat this time, have you?" her mother asked tartly as she made her first sketch.

"I'd need to use a pet, not a stray," Alice replied. "With a stray, you could never be sure what fraction they belonged to."

As the observations continued, she tried to judge the mood of the investigators from the rhythm of their scribbling, the pauses and deliberations. Were they feeling angry, puzzled, vindicated? Timothy had offered no firm predictions; the putative new fraction remained too poorly characterized to be slotted in among the others. But to refute the claim that she had failed in her duties and introduced contamination from Salton or Ridgewood would require both the validity of Timothy's theory and some luck in the specific qualities of the interloper. Only one pair among the three dancing couples could see the anomalous tissue, after all, and two of those pairs would still be consistent with the contamination hypothesis. A further round of inspections a week hence might settle the issue, but that wouldn't be much help for the voters of Myton.

Her father scratched out a line in his notes. What did that mean? Alice watched him adjust the focus on his microscope, turning the knob that raised and lowered the barrel. Would he lie about his observations, just to protect his reputation? Just to delay his theory's demise? Why couldn't she have been born of stone, so she could take her place beside each of the six in turn, and see exactly what they saw?

When the notebooks had been gathered, Alice hung back, reluctant to accept them. All the note-takers shed skin on the coarse sheets of fibrous minerals that served as the books' pages; you only had to slide a finger across their surface to suffer an abrasion. She thought she'd taken all the necessary precautions when preparing the slides, but wasn't it more likely that she'd been careless than that the results were pointing to the true nature of the disease? She'd mounted the samples of her own flesh a day after she'd dealt with Timothy's; that alone could explain why one set was clean, and the other was not.

"Are you going to do this, or should I find someone else?" her mother asked.

"I'll do it."

Alice carried the books to her workroom. No more delaying the verdict—and no denials or excuses if she turned out to be at fault. She needed to be as honest as she wanted the investigators themselves to be.

She opened her own notebook and started tabulating the results, transcribing and collating without interpreting anything, leaving the key that revealed the true identity of each slide locked in the drawer of her desk. She'd contemplated shuffling the notebooks themselves and trying to disguise the authors' names, but she knew everyone's handwriting too well; all she could do was hum to herself and try to interrupt her train of thought whenever she found herself dwelling on the question of whether she'd seen enough of the results yet to decode their significance and know if the weight of evidence had started leaning either way.

When she was done—when it was too late to pause and contemplate the pros and cons of falsifying the results, if only for long enough to send her father back to Myton to intervene in the vote—she unlocked the drawer and took out the list she'd used to renumber the slides.

Decoded, the results made it clear that her own dead flesh was starting to disperse; though Mr Warren and her mother had seen it most clearly, the other four observers had also noticed traces of it. Timothy's flesh had shared the same fate; everyone could see it to some degree.

But the strange specks from the last round of observations, that only Mr Warren of Salton and Mr Grevell of Ridgewood had seen, were invisible to both men now, as well as to their current dance partners.

It was Mr Pemberthy and Mrs Bambridge who had sketched them, in more or less the same locations as their predecessors.

Alice closed her eyes, too shaken to feel anything like relief, not even sure yet exactly what this told her. Once she would have claimed, on evidence like this, that the diseased tissue had "moved between the fractions", but Timothy's way of thinking made that sound absurd.

It was Mr Warren and Mr Grevell who had moved on, going their separate ways to the other two interaction regions. The specks of tissue had not; they had stayed behind, to be found by the latest pair of visitors.

But if she followed the dance back in time, who had lingered beneath the same spotlight before them? She knew the interactions themselves by heart, but that wasn't enough to answer the question. She dug up her notes on Timothy's formulas, and sat for a while, checking and rechecking her conclusions.

Timothy himself had been in the same interaction region when the sample was taken. The interloper couldn't have stayed still, but it hadn't really joined the wider dance at all. Somehow it was weaving a path that constrained it to the four dimensions of a single region, patiently waiting to embrace whoever came within its reach.

12

Alice sat on a bench beside the sculpture that greeted travelers on their way into Ryther, reassured by the shape of the lopsided pyramid that the meeting she was hoping for might yet eventuate. All the girders still appeared equally solid; if she'd been looking at the structure for the first time, she would have had no way of guessing which of them belonged to which fraction.

She spotted her father approaching, hurrying along the road. She rose and waved to him, unsure if she should run to meet him. He raised his hand, and she thought she detected a smile.

"What's the news?" she called out to him, when she judged he was in earshot.

"They're ending the isolation!" he announced. "It was close…but still decisive!"

Alice began walking toward him. "Congratulations!" She felt a twinge of shame at all the accusations she'd hurled against him in the past. In the end, he really did care about the truth; it had just taken a while to convince him.

When they met up, he glanced toward the sculpture before quickly embracing her, then they set off toward the town together.

"Did Mr Watkins gloat terribly?" she asked.

"He seemed rather pleased with himself about the vote," her father replied, "but I'm afraid he was every bit as skeptical about our observations here as he was about my theory of cross-fractional pollution."

"And Mrs Kenworth?"

"Entirely unswayed, as you'd imagine."

"But the vote is the vote?" Alice asked warily. "She won't have any choice but to accept it?"

"She certainly can't stop anyone leaving Myton. I wouldn't put it past her supporters to harass visitors, though, so we do need to warn all our neighbors that they'd be wise to proceed cautiously. Maybe in a few months' time we'll start holding fairs again, but we can't expect everything to go back to the way it was overnight."

"No." Alice laughed, and raised her face toward the sun. "It's progress, though, isn't it?" She'd been harboring an extravagant fantasy in which all of the towns in the region began hosting groups of investigators just like the one in Ryther. It was clearly premature to hope that Myton could join in such a scheme, but that didn't preclude all the rest. With the isolation over, and the Dispersion beginning to yield its secrets, what better way to hasten its demise than to subject it to even more scrutiny?

Her father said something she couldn't quite make out; she looked toward him and saw that he was starting to fade.

"Don't worry, I'll chaperone you in!" she shouted. They were both wearing rings and bracelets; he could follow behind her confident that she'd divert any passerby they encountered who might otherwise risk a mutually injurious colocation.

"Very well," he bellowed back. His voice now was not at all like he'd sounded from a distance; the diminution of his interactions with the fraction of the air that could affect her ears seemed to thin out some overtones more than others, giving it an unsettlingly reedy timbre.

She walked slowly into town, glancing back often to check that he was keeping up with her, and to ensure that she had a clear sense of the area behind her that she needed to protect. A few people they passed glared at them censoriously, but said nothing and kept a respectful distance. Alice couldn't blame them for disapproving, but she'd begged her father to return with news of the vote as soon as possible, so it was more her fault than his that the timing had turned out so precariously.

Once she'd escorted Mr Pemberthy to his lodgings, she made her way to the hospital. In the corridor, she saw Mr Bolton, Timothy's father, emerging from the ward.

"Alice," he greeted her. His voice was flat. "Do you have to see him now? He's not in a good way."

"I could come back later," she said.

"Maybe it's time to stop," he suggested.

"Stop what?"

"Coming back."

Alice hesitated. Mr Bolton said, "It's spread to his lungs. It hurts for him to breathe now, let alone speak. He might have a few days left, but he's not going to be in a state to hold a conversation."

Alice refused to weep in front of this man; it felt like it would be a kind of trespass, trampling over his own grief. "You should know how much his ideas are helping us," she said. "Without them, we'd be completely in the dark."

Mr Bolton nodded distractedly, as if this was as meaningless to him as any other attempt at consolation. "He wrote some things that he wanted you to have. The nurses can give them to you."

"Thank you."

DISPERSION

Alice went to the nurses' station and waited, not wanting to interrupt anyone in the middle of their duties on the ward. She was angry at herself at how unprepared she'd been for this moment; she'd seen the same abrupt decline in too many other people to claim to be surprised. Had she really thought the six could unravel the whole problem fast enough to develop a cure for him? Even with the insights he'd given them, nothing could happen so swiftly.

She caught a nurse's eye and explained what she was seeking. The pages had been kept with their roots in water, and Timothy's words still looked fresh on the woven reeds.

She read the new notes as she walked back to the warehouse; there were a few calculations, but many more pages of exposition, speculation and advice. "We need to remember that all these formulas describe an idealized motion, but the real trajectory of inanimate matter spreads out from it like a wave. And yet living things have taken that idealized path and made it the target of their strategy: they acquire and discard new material as needed to keep themselves close to the path, even as the laws of nature at the deepest level try to tear them away from it. This strange organism you have discovered must have a strategy of its own, perhaps as old as the fractions we are familiar with. And if that's true, perhaps the reason we have never suffered from this disease before is because the animalcule itself has never suffered from it either. If it is making us sick now, perhaps that is because it, too, has grown sick."

Alice turned that over in her mind, trying to flesh it out into something more than poetry. An organism that succeeded in keeping itself within a single interaction region could not infect any ordinary creature for long; if it could not live freely, the best it could hope for would be to find a new host of a different fraction. But the human fractions, even at the best of times, did not intermingle sufficiently to make that a viable modus operandi.

In other species of animals, the fractions were still attuned to the dangers of colocation, but the geographical partitioning was far less rigid. So perhaps the interloper's natural home was the body of a bird, a fox, a dragonfly, where it might well be carried on the wind from one branch of the sixfold family tree to another, without the need to single out an especially cosmopolitan victim.

But then how had it managed to ravage Timothy's body for month after month? There were only two answers Alice could conceive of: either there were a multitude of different infective agents, spread across all three interaction regions, entering and leaving the host in turn. Or the specks they had seen in the slides were not behaving as they had when they were surrounded by living tissue. To infect the host for more than a few days, they'd need to follow it from region to region.

Alice sat in her workroom, rereading the notes. Timothy had found one possible solution for the idealized path the interloper could be clinging to—at least in the form in which they were observing it, trapped beside his dead tissue in the slides. But the truth was, they were still in the dark about the most important things: how had it remained inside his body for so long, and why had it done so much damage when it finally broke free?

She put the sheets down and started sobbing, covering her mouth to stifle the sound, even though her closest neighbors had no hope of hearing her.

13

Alice woke to a pounding on the door. She lifted her head from the desk, confused for a moment about where she was. From the gloom she judged it to be early evening; she must have fallen asleep. She should have been at home cooking dinner, but her mother would not have come to seek her out like this.

"Who is it?" she called, as she lit a lamp. There was no reply, but the banging continued. She opened the door to find, hanging in midair, a lamp that appeared unlit to her, and a slate, bearing the words, "Fire in town. I can smell it."

Alice grabbed her own slate and followed the visitant out onto the street; she finally got a better look at the slate with the message, and concluded from the familiar pattern of cracks around the frame that it was her father's.

"Where?" she muttered to herself, hurrying behind him as he followed the scent of Mytonian smoke, willing him to be mistaken. Who knew what strange olfactory phantoms might arise in the wake of the transition?

The streets were crowded with people on their way to dine, or visit with friends; Alice caught their amused expressions at the bobbing slate that weaved around them rather more closely than was decorous, but at least Mr Pemberthy himself was now harmless.

They began to cross the square, but then her father halted. "Tavern," he wrote. "I can't go any closer."

Alice gazed in the direction they'd been walking. There were three taverns on the far side of the square, and they all appeared perfectly intact.

"Which one?" she wrote. "From our left?"

He paused. How thick was the smoke, that he couldn't reply immediately? Finally, he wrote, "Second."

Alice ran, pushing her way through the throng. When she entered the tavern the sound of laughter and chatter around her was deafening; she looked around and saw a man carrying a plate to one of the tables.

"Excuse me," she begged, grabbing his elbow.

"Could you wait your turn, please," he replied, more patiently than she had any right to expect.

"There's a fire! You need to get everyone out!"

That caught his attention, but he demanded, "Where?"

"I'm not sure," Alice confessed. "It's Mytonian. It could be anywhere. It could be all around us!"

She watched the man's expression change from confusion to skepticism. "How could you possibly know that?"

Alice fought to stay calm; even if news of the isolation's end had spread, visitors would hardly be expected so soon. "I have a Mytonian guest."

"And he set this fire?"

"No! But he can smell it, and see it. He pointed it out from a distance, but it's too fierce for him to join me."

The man remained undecided, frowning at this bizarre claim but not quite ready to dismiss it. Alice supposed she sounded like a madwoman or a prankster—or perhaps some kind of troublemaker, aiming to bring their neighbors into disrepute at the very moment they had voted to restore a normal relationship.

She said, "Maybe if you put your hand to something? One of the tables?"

He walked over to an empty table, set down the plate he'd been carrying, and pressed his palm hard against the stone. "It does feel a bit warm," he admitted. "Warmer than it ought to be." He was still hesitant. Hadn't he ever seen the famous trick, as a child? When the conjuror let you touch the stone plate, you noticed it was just a little bit warm—and then a minute later, it was in pieces?

Apparently, he had.

"Ladies and gentlemen!" he shouted. "I need to ask everyone to leave the establishment now, in an orderly fashion. There is a fire we need to deal with, and while it's small and contained for the moment, we can not risk your safety by allowing you to remain. There will be free meals to compensate for the disruption, which I'll be honored to provide on any night that suits you, but for now, please, I must ask you to leave."

Alice felt her body sag with relief as the grumbling patrons began to file out. The "small fire" was a clever lie; by the time they'd convinced all these people that they were the target of Mytonian saboteurs the whole town could have burned to the ground.

"What now?" the landlord asked Alice, as if she had some kind of experience with these matters. "Can I put it out with rainwater? Or sand? Sand should work!"

"I can't advise you," she said. "But trying to fight this, blind…?" She spread her hands in resignation. "I'm sorry." She didn't want the man to lose his business, but she wasn't going to stand here passing buckets of sand to him while they waited to see if the roof would cave in.

It took her forever to find her father again. His slate was bobbing awkwardly around the square, caught between flows of people—many of whom seemed to have been attracted by the commotion, only to linger for the sole purpose of expressing their disappointment at the lack of any visible conflagration.

"The tavern's been evacuated," she wrote on her own slate.

"Good," he replied.

"Who would do this?" Alice wrote. The question was rhetorical, but her bewilderment was sincere. For all her fretting over the extremists who'd cheered Mrs Kenworth, she had never imagined them acting so swiftly, or with such callous intent.

"They must have left before I did," her father wrote. "Prepared even before the vote was announced."

They'd known they were going to lose, but they were committed to their position regardless. But what did they imagine the outcome of their actions would be? The people of Ryther, and the other four towns, would just surrender their land and walk away, leaving Myton with a magical moat of wilderness that would protect it from the Dispersion?

"How much fuel, do you think?" she asked her father.

"About as much as a dozen people could have carried," he replied, getting to the heart of the question. Not a vast army, but not a mere handful either. A dozen invisible saboteurs could not wipe a town off the map, but they could harm a great many people, and stir up a lot of ill will against their home town.

There was a loud creaking sound from across the square. Alice turned just in time to see the tavern collapse in on itself, spilling rubble onto the street and sending up a dust cloud to rival the smoke that her father must have been seeing all along.

The spectators were silent for a moment, but then they began shouting at each other in astonishment. It would not take long for the whole of Ryther to learn that this was not the work of a small fire that had somehow wrought damage disproportionate to its size.

"Follow me back?" Alice suggested. She wasn't expecting the tavern's patrons to try to stone their invisible benefactor to death, but it still seemed wise to err on the side of caution: the mere presence of his disembodied slate was potentially inflammatory now, and the crowd was subject to whatever rumors and speculation gained the most traction in the next few minutes.

They made their way back to the warehouse without any further exchange of messages, but when they were safely indoors Alice asked, "What should we do? Can Myton rein these people in?"

"Perhaps." Her father hesitated, his chalk poised but motionless. "I should go back and spread word of their crimes," he wrote finally. "Mr Warren can serve as fire warden."

Alice replied, "Very well." Given that Mr Warren had apparently slept through the blaze, she would have felt safer with her father on fire watch, but no other emissary would be taken as seriously in Myton.

"Please tell your mother where I've gone."

"Of course."

He put down the slate, and Alice saw the door to the street swing open. When he was gone, she stood for a while, trying to find the most favorable light in which to view the night's events. The saboteurs had failed to inflict a single casualty. Their grand gesture had simply exposed them, and would soon see everyone they'd hoped to intimidate taking steps to defend themselves.

Before leaving, she went to each of the other investigators and explained what had happened; all but Mr Warren, whose town was safe for the next few days, chose to depart at once to carry word back to their homes.

As Mrs Bambridge packed for her journey, she reassured Alice, "They're not going to make trouble for anyone but themselves. Their own townspeople voted against them!"

Alice smiled, welcoming the optimistic appraisal, but a part of her mind was racing ahead, cranking out scenarios that had surely occurred to their enemy already. *Come at night, and hide a stone knife in the gutter. In the morning, when the town square is full of people, retrieve the weapon and stab the air a dozen times; you're sure to hit at least one person in the crowd before anyone notices the act of levitation. Drop the knife, and vanish.*

What could be simpler?

For the perpetrator: no witnesses, no risk of capture or punishment.

For the victims: no defense.

14

Alice's mother ascended the ramp to the stage, leaning on Alice's arm to keep her balance as she made her way to the lectern. "We have a proposal from Myton," she announced. "Twelve monitors, twelve volunteers, willing to give up their time and the comforts of home to live among us and help keep us safe."

"And who keeps us safe from them?" a man shouted. He was not a lone dissenter; Alice could see other members of the gathering nodding in agreement.

Rebecca paused and looked around the hall, clearly bewildered by the response she was receiving. "Why would anyone treat that offer with suspicion? If they meant us harm, they wouldn't ask permission to join us! And they will all be vetted—"

"Vetted by your husband?" a woman interjected. "The instigator of the isolation?"

"Vetted by everyone of good will in Myton!" Rebecca retorted.

"Everyone *claiming* good will," the same woman countered.

Rebecca began mumbling obscenities under her breath. Alice touched her arm, but she was not in a mood to be pacified.

"This is a sign of both friendship and enlightened self-interest," she argued. "Everyone in Myton knows that these attacks risk undermining their own safety, and the prosperity they were hoping the end of the isolation would bring. Why should we doubt that these people are opposed to the fanatics who are trying to rob them of their future?"

When Rebecca ceded the lectern, Mrs Collins, the interjector, took her place. "Here is an alternative proposal that we should be taking to our neighbors: each of the five towns that are in danger should send volunteers to the other four, so we will always have friendly eyes among us who can spot the saboteurs from Myton."

"Four times more people, four times more organizing, four times the delay!" Rebecca yelled up at her.

"Four times as safe!" Mrs Collins shouted back.

"No it's not," Rebecca said, simply confused now, as if she couldn't quite believe that anyone could reason so poorly about the situation.

Other people in the audience took up the chant. "Four times as safe! Four times as safe!"

There was no time to organize a vote from the whole town; it was up to the elected councilors to decide on their behalf. Alice sat beside her mother, trying to keep her from being drawn into futile shouting matches with her opponents, while the council, having retired to their chambers, discussed the proposal among themselves.

"I should never have sent you to Myton," her mother declared gloomily.

"Why's that?"

"If the vote had gone in favor of isolation, at least the extremists would have been half-satisfied. That might have kept them in check."

Alice decided this was a roundabout way of telling her that she should not have begged her father to go back to try to sway the vote. "Hindsight is a wonderful thing," she replied. "Maybe you should have just kidnapped him before he walked out on us the first time, and then all this hysteria about maintaining the purity of the fractions might have been nipped in the bud."

Her mother laughed dryly. "All right, I deserved that." She reached down to massage her knee, wincing. "I do wish I hadn't followed you up into the hills, though. I've been paying for that ever since."

The councilors filed back into the public gallery.

"We have given all submissions our earnest and careful consideration," the Mayor assured the gathering. "And we have decided to send emissaries to Salton, Drayville, Bonnerton and Ridgewood, to negotiate an exchange of monitors between the towns during this period of heightened tension. Volunteers for this initiative are welcome, and in the coming days we will be making further announcements as to how they can apply, and what selection criteria they should address in their written applications."

Rebecca said, "Hooray."

15

"You can have my dirty bandages," Mrs Jasper decided. "That's all. You're not cutting me, like you did to that poor boy!"

"No, of course not. Thank you for helping." Alice's face burned, but she persisted. "If you'd be willing to let us have samples of urine and stools…?"

"That's disgusting!"

"It is, but if we find something it will be worth it."

Mrs Jasper said, "So long as the nurses just hand it over to you from the bedpan. So long as I don't have to watch you dealing with it." She grimaced. "What are you going to find, poking around in that filth?"

"If we knew the answer, we wouldn't have to do it," Alice replied.

"Fair enough."

Alice left the ward, exhausted, with consent for a supply of noninvasive samples from eight of the twelve patients. No one had agreed to let her take tissue or draw blood, but why would they? It had done Timothy no good.

Back in her workroom, she began preparing slides from the bandages of three patients with the Dispersion, and three with other kinds of wounds. Even if they couldn't catch the disease at work within the body, the detritus it left behind could help them winnow down the possibilities.

Her mother knocked on the door and entered without waiting for an invitation. "Apparently someone's started planting wooden spikes on all the trails leading down from the hills," she said.

"I don't understand," Alice replied. "If the saboteurs can't see them, how will they be injured?"

"The rumor is the stake-planters bought some chickens from Haverfield, and they're smearing small, sharp stones in the excrement and embedding them in the tips of the stakes."

"That's...creative, I suppose." Alice had trouble deciding whether the intruders would face a real risk of injury and sepsis, or if the end result would just be someone kicking a malodorous speck of gravel aside. But she had more urgent things to ponder.

DISPERSION

"How is it that I exist?" she asked her mother.

"I thought we had that conversation a while ago."

"Not one trace of my father's emission could persist inside you—but he's still my father, as surely as if he were from Ryther. So in the end, his contribution was not material at all, but purely in the nature of information."

"Yes." Rebecca pursed her lips with mock-solemnity. "When you put it as starkly as that, it's quite unnerving. It's as if you could find yourself carrying a child just from reading the wrong kind of poetry."

Alice laughed, but she persisted. "Your body transcribed… something. At the very least, whatever it was that gave me some resemblance to him, in my appearance and character. But is that all? We know that paternal inheritance is not constrained to superficial matters: there are ailments that a father can pass on to his child, despite the mother being in perfect health."

"Which means the father's body can offer bad advice sometimes," Rebecca concluded. "Should that surprise us?"

Alice said, "No, but why heed it? If the mother is healthy and the father is not, why does she pass the bad advice on to her child?"

"You might as well ask why anyone suffers from any sickness, ever," Rebecca replied. "Why don't we all just find someone healthy and imitate them perfectly, down to the bones? Easy to talk about, not so easily done."

"But if there ever was a chance to do that, surely it would be at conception? When it comes to creating a child, there is no other source of guidance but the imitation of the parents—so why not imitate the mother alone?"

"What if she's not healthy, though? What if she's the one with the ailment? What happens in the womb isn't driven by some omniscient force—or even by the mother's own insights. I might *know* that I have some heritable illness that has passed down the maternal line in my family...but is that inference available to guide my reproductive system? The same reproductive system, more or less, as possessed by animals with no notion of anything so abstract as a familial disease."

"That makes sense," Alice conceded. "So the body has no choice but to gamble, mixing up advice from both parents in the hope that the child will stand a better chance of good health than it would if there were a universal rule that committed it to mimicking the mother or father alone."

Rebecca concurred. "From both the breeding of livestock, and what we see in human families, it's clear that there's an equal contribution from both parents."

"And there's no reason for that to be different if the father belongs to a different fraction than the mother?"

Rebecca said, "I don't think so. At the time of conception—if conception is possible at all—the body can't tell the difference. And it's not unknown for farmers to pay for the use of prize bulls from other towns to introduce traits into their herds."

Alice was still groping her way forward, but she had a clearer picture now of where she was heading. "If the instructions to the child's body come equally from both parents, and if the parents need not even be from the same fraction, then we must all—inasmuch as we are healthy—be performing identical actions. Whatever fraction we belong to, the processes we use to keep ourselves in that fraction—to resist the kind of dispersion that afflicts inanimate objects—must be the same."

Rebecca was bewildered. "I don't know what you mean by 'the same.' A Rytheran gut absorbs Rytheran food; a Mytonian gut absorbs Mytonian food."

"You said the womb has no abstract knowledge of its owner's ancestry," Alice replied. "Still less then, surely, does a Rytheran gut, or lung, or liver know that it's Rytheran. We must all be following identical rules, which only work to different effect because the organ in question is located somewhere different." She resisted the temptation to add: *Not different in the sense of one town or another; different in Timothy's twelve-dimensional space.* "Whatever my body does to keep itself intact must look the same, from its point of view, as whatever a Mytonian body is doing to the same end."

"They both defend themselves in the same manner," Rebecca conceded. "Though I'm not sure why you're making so much of it."

"Because the symmetry between the six fractions is perfect," Alice declared, "but that doesn't mean it was inevitable. I can follow my father's instructions without harm, and it would have been the same were my parentage reversed…or scrambled up in any manner. If you'd come from Bonnerton and he from Drayville, none of it would have made the slightest difference. But for all we know, there might be a village in some distant country whose citizens could not beget children safely with anyone we know, because the instructions *their* children needed to survive would not fulfill the same purpose if enacted within our bodies."

"Umm…perhaps." Rebecca was growing wary again.

"If the Dispersion belongs to a seventh fraction," Alice reasoned, "what *it* needs to do in order to survive, and what *we* need, might bear no resemblance to each other at all. If we transcribe its instructions into our own fraction, we might well carry them along with us, allowing them to remain a part of our flesh—but the result won't be like my own benign parentage. It will be like carrying a child fathered by someone from that mythical village."

Rebecca said, "You've lost me, I'm afraid. You think the victims had sex with goblins, and they're giving birth to the unviable offspring of that forbidden coupling?"

Alice glanced at Timothy's papers. She wanted to say: *It's all in the mathematics, if you look closely enough. Some variables are just names, and you can swap them around without changing a thing. Others are as different as up and down, night and day.*

But to her mother, this was all just book-keeping.

"Never mind," she said. "I don't quite know where I was going, myself. Let me think on it a little longer."

16

At the funeral, Alice kept her distance from Timothy's family. What could she be, in their eyes, but a reminder of the disease that had taken their son and brother from them?

As the mourners left the cemetery, a young man approached Alice. "I think I saw you in the hospital," he said. "You're the medical researcher?"

"Researchers' assistant."

"I'm Christopher."

"Alice." She shook his hand.

"It's good to meet you. Timothy talked about you all the time."

Alice laughed curtly, embarrassed. "I'm glad he had someone to whom he could complain about his tormentor."

"He never thought of you like that," Christopher assured her. "We used to study together, and he was working on his system even then. I was skeptical at first, but then I started to appreciate the beauty of it. It's like trying to understand day and night, and all the seasons, eclipses, transits and occultations while living beneath an overcast sky. You can't ever hope to see what's really going on—but if you ignore what the cycles are trying to tell you, you're certainly the poorer for it."

"He was hoping to be a teacher, wasn't he?" Alice asked.

"Yes. And he would have been a good one. So long as he had time off to travel to meetings of the learned societies." Christopher's tone was admiring, but perhaps a little envious too.

"What's your vocation?"

"I'm a builder." He smiled; maybe he'd caught a flicker of surprise on Alice's face. "What, you don't think a stonemason can love mathematics? I promise you, without geometry you'd be living in ruins."

"Oh, I'm sure that's true." Alice walked beside him in silence for a while. "So you talked about his ideas?"

"All the time."

"What he did was important," she said. "I wish I could persuade more people to see that. I can follow most of what he left me, but not all of it. If I had someone to talk to who didn't treat it all as pointless nonsense..."

Christopher nodded. "I understand. He always thought it would take a lifetime for his ideas to be accepted. The ones who got there sooner need to stick together."

Alice recounted the latest observations that the six had reported. "Whenever the samples were collected, there seem to be traces in them that manage to cling to the interaction region that the patient was in at the time. They can't have always done that, or they would have simply fallen away."

"But if they're constantly trying to do it, and only succeeding now and then, it's that success that will cause them to be shed," Christopher reasoned. "Why do they succeed, though? Or why do they not succeed from the start?"

Alice said, "My belief is that it's like the difference between copying a passage in a book that recommends a certain method for copying passages in a book, and actually following the recommended method to make the copy."

Christopher paused to digest that. "All right."

"Timothy found a formula for what might be a seventh fraction—or maybe a seventh, eighth and ninth. With the usual six, there's a kind of symmetry between them: everything you do as a member of one is just a shifted version of what the others are doing. It's like the reflections in a kaleidoscope; you really can't single one out as special. Any one of them could be the original, and the result would be no different.

"But the new fraction isn't just a reflection of the others; if you want to maintain it, you need to do something genuinely new. Doing what we usually do, we could copy the instructions for that new kind of copying, along with the rest of our flesh, and keep it all intact as we move between the three interaction regions in the usual way. But then, if we get confused somehow between the instructions for our own kind of copying, and these instructions we've been carrying with us by mistake, we might start to actually follow them."

"Ah." Christopher stopped walking and beamed at her. "You do know how much he would have loved that idea?"

Alice thought: *Maybe, but he might have loved it more if I'd thought of it sooner.*

"Somehow we ingest this animalcule when we're both in the same interaction region," Christopher mused, "and we tear it away from its own preferred path, 'repairing' it as we would repair our own flesh when it starts spreading out from its fraction. And our victim is helpless at first: it has no choice but to go along for the ride. But after a while, having clutched it to our bosom, we start to treat it as part of the family, and give it free rein. It's too small to drag our whole bodies onto its path, but when it breaks free, it takes a part of us with it."

"I think that's what's happening," Alice affirmed. "But I don't know how to prove it, let alone devise a remedy."

Christopher thought for a while. "I'm no doctor, I can't help you find a cure. But I'm not afraid of a few sines and cosines, as some of your colleagues seem to be. If this animalcule belongs to an entirely new fraction, then even when it lies in the same interaction region as the two observers who can see it, there ought to be a measurable distinction between the strength of its interaction, and that of material that actually belongs to either of their fractions. If Timothy has already written down a formula, I could help you extract that kind of prediction."

"So...we should measure this thing's resistance to co-location with different materials?" Alice proposed.

Christopher shook his head. "I think that would be a bit too exacting. Why not stick to the method you're already using: visibility. But make it more precise. Take two wedges of some common plant material from Ryther and from Myton, for example, that have been sliced to vary in thickness along their length, so that the two observers can say of the animalcule, 'it hinders the light through the microscope to the same degree as the point on this wedge seven-tenths from the thin end'. If we've worked through the numbers in advance, and lo and behold they agree with the observations, then that will strengthen your hand, won't it?"

"It might."

They'd reached the center of town. "Maybe I can call on you this evening, and we can work through the predictions?" Christopher suggested.

Alice heard shouting from across the square; she turned to see the meeting hall shaking, as if in an earthquake. For a second she thought it had to be another fire like the one in the tavern, but the building hadn't fractured and given way to gravity; rather, it looked as if it was being buffeted by repeated blows.

Christopher let out a series of curses befitting a mason who'd just smashed his own hand. And, injured or not, he'd turned paler than anyone Alice had seen in the hospital wards.

"Are there people on the roof, swinging hammers?" she wondered.

"No one's that strong," he declared. "Not a dozen saboteurs. Not a hundred."

Alice felt something stinging her legs through her trousers. She looked down to see a cloud of grit and small pebbles rushing across the square, far too high above the cobblestones for any gust of wind to have lofted them.

"Run," Christopher said quietly. Then he bellowed the word, gesturing toward the other onlookers with an outstretched arm. "Run!" he repeated, taking just a few steps himself, as if reluctant to leave the square before anyone had heeded him. "Run, you fools, *it's a flood!*" he screamed, then he clutched at Alice and dragged her along with him as he started sprinting back the way they'd come.

She broke free and headed west.

"What are you doing?" he yelled.

"My mother…!"

"You don't have time!"

Alice raised her hands resignedly and turned away from him, then she ran with all her strength, heading for the warehouse, her vision shrinking to the path ahead. When people crossed in front of her, she shouted, "Flood!" but she didn't pause to see if her words had roused them into action. Unless they were dazed by the dreamlike sight of stone tools and household goods flying by, they probably didn't need her warning.

The detritus swirled in eddies around her shins, showing signs of starting to settle; maybe the first rush of water from the north had passed now. But once the wave rose up the opposite side of the valley, the slope would send most of it back down again. Like a tooth pushed first one way and then the other, many walls that hadn't fallen with the first assault would succumb to the second.

As she approached the warehouse, it was still standing. She ran to the nearest entrance and tugged on the door, but some hydraulic force opposed her.

"Mother!" she called, but there was no answer.

She moved to the window and peered inside. One of the benches in the hexagon had shifted, and she could see pieces of glassware bobbing above the floor, but there was no one in sight. Out of habit, she looked toward the clock. There was a transition due to start in a matter of minutes: the Saltonian fraction would begin to interact with the Rytheran.

She'd made a mistake in coming here; whatever the source of the water, two of the six would have known what was happening much sooner than she had. Everyone would have fled while she was still on her way; they must have recruited some bystander to help carry her mother.

If the water was Saltonian they'd already know, and they'd be acting accordingly. But she had no way to tell. Was the timing pure coincidence, and the risk just a matter of collapsing walls and water-borne objects? Or was everyone whose feet weren't dry about to get a lesson in colocation?

Alice took her shoes off and tossed them onto the roof of the warehouse, then began climbing up the down-pipe that drained the gutter. The stone was cold and slippery beneath her toes, as if the phantom water was already lapping across the narrowing gulf to touch her skin.

She was breathless when she reached the eaves, and her hands were bleeding. She stretched back with one arm and caught hold of the edge of the roof; the curved pieces that formed the bed of the gutter shifted precariously beneath her fingers.

She tried a different handhold; the structure felt more secure. She leaned out, testing it with more of her weight, then pushed herself away from the down-pipe and grabbed at the roof with her other hand.

As she was hauling herself up, she heard stone smashing against stone, and people screaming in the distance. With the bottom of her rib cage still pressed against the gutter, she looked out across the south side of town, and saw a house three streets away topple. Rubble spewed out from the broken structure, defying gravity, crashing into a neighbor's wall.

She drew her legs up and huddled against the roof of the warehouse, her teeth chattering either from fear or from some motion in the tiles beneath her.

The building shuddered. Alice clawed at the tiles, dizzy from anticipated movement—but she did not spin away into the deluge, and the walls beneath her did not give way.

She waited, shivering, for something else to happen, and when it didn't she raised herself up on her elbows and turned to look down into the street.

Something dazzled her eyes; she squinted and reduced it to a patch of brightness, rocking back and forth. Sunlight was glinting off the surface, but the water was still only half-present. Under pressure, it would push deep into Rytheran flesh—but it could no longer come and go from their bodies unfelt, without consequence.

In the streets around her, the screams were growing louder.

17

The shelter was full of rumors. "The Saltonians must have had a hand in it, too," Alice heard a fellow volunteer insist. "Their observers reported nothing! Their workers at the dam did nothing! They pretend they're innocent victims like the rest of us, but I know they've made some deal with Myton to carve up the land once they've forced us out."

Alice kept quiet; she'd discovered that the more she argued, the more vehement her interlocutors became. She tried to shut out the noise of paranoia and recrimination, and concentrate on the work at hand.

Many of the amputees had recovered from their surgery enough to start trying out prostheses, with a helper to bear some of their weight and keep them from losing balance. She did her best to facilitate their first steps, trying to take her cues from them as to the pace and amount of support they needed, even when they were too angry and frustrated to spell it out for her moment by moment. There had to be experts in this kind of rehabilitation somewhere, but with hundreds of cases to deal with in a town the size of Ryther, everyone had to improvise. All she could do was try to learn as she went.

Each evening, after her shift, she went back to the warehouse to help her mother sort through the mess. The other researchers had returned to their home towns, hoping to obtain new equipment to replace everything that had been damaged in the flood. Most of the broken instruments were beyond repair, but many of the notebooks could still be reassembled or copied. The information had not all been lost.

"I don't know why we're bothering," Rebecca declared, rummaging through a pile of salvaged pages. The water had transformed the crisp lines of the words into dark bruises and broken veins. "Nobody cares what the truth is about the Dispersion."

"They will when we have the whole story," Alice replied. "They'll care once we can offer them a cure."

"Are you sure? Or will they only believe that it's a cure if it suits them?"

"If a member of your family is dying—"

"If a member of your family is dying, you're the luckiest person in the world. You have a weapon that excuses any exercise of your passions, however unrelated it might be to the actual cause of the affliction."

Alice bit her tongue. Rebecca needed to give voice to her disappointment, but she would never abandon the work.

"Your father dropped in this afternoon. He brought some glassware from Myton."

"Is he still here?"

"No, he returned straight away. He's trying to drum up support for us among the merchants there, which apparently entails an endless succession of tedious dinner parties."

"How are things in Myton?" Alice wondered. "Parties aside."

"There've been three murders," Rebecca replied bluntly. "The deaths in plain sight, but the assassins unseen."

"Retribution against random strangers." Alice struggled to remain composed; a part of her wanted to cheer. Part of her was happy that innocent people were dying for no reason, just as they had in Ryther. "That's obscene," she said. "And it's only going to make things harder here. How can we expect Myton to police the militias, when we're not doing the same to our own?"

"Ah, but *our* militias are forcing the Mytonians to set their house in order. That's a fair and proportionate response, and any reaction to it is just a vicious escalation." It took a moment for Alice to be sure that her mother was being sarcastic.

The lamp whose light they were working by was wavering, and they had no more fuel on hand.

"We can come back in the morning," Alice suggested. "Once it's light."

"All right."

We won't be stopped, Alice promised herself, as they made their way along the dark streets toward the lodging house. The dam was guarded around the clock; the same weapon could not be used twice. Every town could harass its neighbors with cowardly assassins, every idiot could indulge themselves with wild notions of conspiracy. In the gloom, she could see the real enemy clearly: in the twelve-dimensional ballroom, spinning above the shadows it cast, trapped in a dance it had never wished to join.

Don't worry, she assured it. *I haven't forgotten you. Give me time, and I'll set us both free.*

18

"You're a hard man to find," Alice joked, as she stepped gingerly across the rubble. "Did you get any of my messages?"

"There's a lot to be done," Christopher replied brusquely, and continued chiseling.

Alice nodded, and glanced around the site. He seemed to have only a single apprentice working with him, a girl who looked about half her own age. "People need shelter. I'm only asking for a minute or two to pick your brains."

He put down the hammer and regarded her impatiently. "In all of Ryther, you can't find a real mathematician?"

"I spoke to some of the teachers," she said. "They know the same rote transformations as I do, but they have no intuition for what Timothy was doing."

Christopher wiped his forehead with his sleeve then turned away from her to expel dust from his nostrils. "I don't remember everything I said to you after the funeral, but I was probably just boasting. Trying to live up to his memory, if that makes any sense. His intuition died with him; we won't see it again."

Alice chose her words carefully. "I don't expect you to step into his shoes, but that one conversation we had already helped to make things clearer. I'm not asking you to give me all your time, and I'm not trying to put the weight of this on you. Just give me a few more pushes in the right direction, and tell me if I'm going wildly off course."

Christopher stared at the rubble, and for a moment Alice thought she'd lost him. Then he said, "You know I'm living with my parents? And you have the address?"

"Yes."

"Can you come around this evening? Around eight?"

"I'll be there."

19

Christopher's parents' house was high on the western slope. The whole neighborhood had escaped damage, but as Alice looked down in the moonlight, she had a sweeping view of the course the floodwater had taken when it gouged its way across the valley. She guessed that about one building in five in the water's path had been lost, and a tenth of the population permanently injured. If the people who'd done this believed they were sparing their families from the ravages of the Dispersion, they were already culpable for their own stupidity—but if they'd merely used that as a pretext, what other strange poison had filled their minds? How was it possible to hate your all-but-identical neighbors with even more intensity than you would if they were actually causing holes to appear in your flesh?

The windows of the house were dark, but when she knocked Christopher appeared, carrying a lamp. "Everyone else is asleep," he said quietly. That would have been strange once, but Alice didn't press him for an explanation; either they were weary for a hundred possible reasons, or they were simply conserving fuel. "We can use my mother's study."

Alice took off her shoes and carried them as she followed him through the house. In the study, she placed the bundle of notes she'd brought on the table as he fixed the lamp in place.

"A minute or two?" he asked skeptically, gesturing at the size of the pile.

"Think of that as my reference library," Alice explained. "I'm sure we won't need it all, but I can't say in advance which parts I might have to consult."

Christopher nodded and rubbed his eyes. "All right. Tell me how I can help you."

Alice said, "It looks as if we'll be starting our work again soon, but we've had so many setbacks that I want to be sure we make the best use of our time. When we spoke before, you suggested that you might be able to predict some changes in the visibility of the disease agent, which would be different for the two observers who were able to see it at any given time."

"I remember. You've brought Timothy's notes on the seventh trajectory?"

"Yes." Alice had made three copies; one had survived the flood.

She handed over the pages, and Christopher set to work. She watched him in silence, deciding not to quiz him about his methods for now; it might save them both time in the long run if he could teach her exactly what he was doing, but that could wait until he was feeling less besieged by all his other obligations.

When he'd finished, she looked over the results, and checked that her interpretation of the formulas was correct.

"That was easier than I thought," she admitted.

"Are we done?" he asked, not rudely, but he'd probably been at work since dawn.

"Thank you." Alice hesitated. "I did want to tell you something, though. It's just an idea I had, and you can make of it what you will."

"Go ahead." He rested his chin on his hand, not quite closing his eyes.

"I want to lure it out," she said. "Instead of it taking the victim's flesh, I want to offer it a sacrificial bait."

Christopher said nothing. Behind him, she could see his mother's collection of treatises on classical geometry stacked up on the shelves, probably the only copies in all of Ryther. If they'd been any lower in the valley, they might have been lost in the flood.

Just when Alice was starting to wonder if he'd fallen asleep, he replied, "You want to feed the patient empty food? Stuff them full of...whatever other fraction they can take in at the time?"

"Yes."

"But why do you suppose that the animalcule would prefer that to the patient's own flesh?"

Alice said, "Because of what you said about the visibility. Just because we can't tell the difference between those two fractions for most of the interaction period, it doesn't mean the animalcule will treat them identically."

Christopher massaged his temples. "But that's after it's broken free. When it's inside us, we've copied it the same way we copy our own flesh. We've remade it in our own image."

"We've remade what it's made of, but not what it does," Alice argued. "At the very point where it starts to make trouble, it also starts being different from us again." As she heard her own words she wondered if they were empty rhetoric; maybe she'd convinced herself that they made sense through the sheer power of wishful thinking.

Christopher seemed to be struggling with the same question. "It's possible," he finally conceded. "Though right now, I wouldn't know how to begin to quantify it."

"That's all right. Just...?"

He opened his eyes fully. “Just think about it? Now that you’ve infected me, do I have any choice? At the back of my mind when I’m trying to sleep, on the building site tomorrow when I’m shaping a block, the voice you’ve planted in my skull will be asking: how can we make this work?”

20

Alice rose early, ate a quick breakfast, then wrapped a scarf around her face up to the bridge of her nose and set out for the shelter.

But she'd left it too late to make the journey in comfort; the Dust Army was already out in force. They seemed to be growing in number every day; with their own faces shrouded in fabric, they marched back and forth across the town square, shaking bags of rubble they'd pillaged from the broken houses, or banging together slabs of whatever chalky mineral they'd been able to get their hands on.

Alice understood their reasoning, but the morning light slanting through the airborne motes made it look as if Ryther was trapped forever in the moment after a cataclysm to rival those it had actually endured. It was not that this scene brought back memories of the flood; there were no swirling liquid eddies in the haze of fine grit. But even when she set aside her visceral reaction to the ambience of perpetual ruin, it did not make her feel safe. The hint of visibility it threatened to induce in any would-be assassin cut both ways: if they could be seen, they in turn could also see their victims.

There was nothing to be done but to take shallow breaths and try to keep the grit out of her lungs. She hurried across the square, raising a forearm to her nostrils when she encountered the most noxious and abrasive clouds, for which the scarf proved inadequate.

Halfway to the shelter, she froze: she was sure she'd glimpsed a lacuna weaving its way among the solid pedestrians. Why was no one else alarmed? She jostled for a better vantage, wondering if the people closer to the intruder were blinded by their proximity.

There, again! A head carved out of the dust, like a glass figurine come to life, had passed by above the Rytheran shoulders. The investigators were all confined to the warehouse, only leaving in the presence of chaperones; the monitors from the four towns were required to wear jewel-encrusted sashes that the councilors believed no impostor could afford to imitate. Whoever walked unseen and unheralded through the town was not a friend.

"Who's that?" she called out, removing her scarf and repeating the words, pointing, hoping that someone else would confirm the sighting. People glanced toward her and followed her gaze.

"I see him, I see him!" a man replied. He was carrying a stone knife, which he brandished excitedly; he pushed through the crowd, who recoiled from his weapon as he closed in on the intruder.

Other bystanders around Alice began shouting and gesturing, guiding the man toward his target. "There! No, left—backward!" But Alice had lost sight of the absence; maybe the intruder had been nimble enough to find someone to colocate with, sketched out in the dust like a suit of clothes into which they could step. Even if their double was carrying a weapon, they could adjust their own movements to accommodate the obstacle.

Or maybe even seize it.

"They're going for your knife!" she screamed, with no evidence at all, just hoping that everyone at risk of her imagined strategy would now be forewarned to resist. She could see people clutching at their blades and bludgeons, raising them high into the air, as if they could already sense a competitor reaching for the handle.

Alice closed her eyes and swayed, letting the sounds of panic and anger wash over her. If she shouted the right words, maybe half the crowd would plunge their knives into their own chests, triumphantly rooting out the enemy within, glad to pay the price to save their fellow citizens.

The tone of the hubbub changed abruptly. She opened her eyes; people were laughing. A member of the Dust Army, draped like a ghost, was clapping their chalk blocks together high above their head, and in the white cloud the outlines of an owl hovered, annoyed, shaking the dirt off its feathers.

21

"You need to do the analysis," Alice told her mother. "I don't trust myself anymore."

Rebecca was dubious. "You know I don't follow all this trigonometry. I can understand a normal equation, but this formula you've used is like a string tied in knots."

"That's not important," Alice insisted. "Christopher and I have worked out the predictions; all you need to do is check and see if the numbers people are reporting come close."

"But why? Why don't you trust yourself?"

"It's not that I'd ever lie deliberately," Alice stressed, though even as she said the words she wasn't sure that they were true. "But I might be swayed in a certain direction. If there are any close calls, I might favor one side."

"And you think I'm immune to that?"

Alice smiled. "Maybe not, but I'm not going to tell you which samples are which until you've finished the analysis. You have no way of knowing how I numbered the slides. Not unless you want to fight me for this." She held up the sole key to the drawer that held the list, threaded on a chain around her neck.

"This is what it's come to?" Rebecca asked forlornly.

"The first time I mixed up the slides, you said it was a good idea. I'm just trying to be more thorough."

Rebecca stopped arguing, and carried the notebooks away to her workroom. Alice sat beside the bench, looking around the empty hexagon. The jury had voted, impartially; all that remained was the tallying of the votes. She had to be prepared for whatever was coming, even if it crushed all the hope out of her body.

Timothy had been brave, and brilliant, but it hadn't saved his life, and it didn't mean he'd been right about anything. The two of them had been caught up in their own dance, too honest to amount to a seduction, but not as disinterested as she'd pretended it to be. The truth was, she'd been attracted to him, and she'd let him know, because it made it easier to ask him to give her what she wanted. That he'd given her much more should have been a warning. Her mother had thought he was trying to cheat death, but she was more afraid that he'd just been trying to please her.

DISPERSION

Her mother summoned her. "I've subtracted the quantities you gave me from the observations," she said. "But the residues just look like random numbers to me."

Alice said, "Let me get the key."

She returned with the list, and the two of them worked together, sorting the differences into two sets. One set did indeed remain random. The other started off with a run of small values, which continued to remain small.

Rebecca said, "Now I'm starting to think there's some way you could have tricked me."

Alice shook her head. "Didn't I give you the predictions to hold on to, before anyone even looked at these slides?"

"Yes."

"Do you think I could have made the slides myself out of some kind of ersatz blood—into which I'd introduced fake organisms that Mr Grevell and Mrs Collard would observe, somewhat differently, in just the way I wanted them to?"

"If you could, you've mastered some new art that no one else has," Rebecca admitted.

Alice hadn't dared imagine that she'd end the day elated, but she hadn't expected to feel so sick and helpless in victory, as if she'd just been pushed naked into a gladiatorial arena.

"Tell me you believe me," she pleaded. "Tell me I'm not alone with this." Timothy had done his best, but now she needed every ally she could find: she needed Christopher, she needed her mother and her father, she needed all of the six and all of Ryther behind her or she was going to break beneath the weight of it.

Rebecca took her hand and squeezed it. "I believe you. I'm going to have to brush up on my trigonometry before I really understand what we're chasing here—but whatever it is, you've just taken us ten steps closer to defeating it."

22

These people are already wasting away, and you want my permission to put them on a diet that will rob them of any hope of maintaining what little flesh they've been able to retain?" Dr Harvey did not seem hostile, or even disrespectful, but it was clear that he found the group's proposal transparently absurd, if not homicidal.

Alice kept silent; her official function in the meeting was to take notes. Her mother had brought Mrs Bambridge along, as the currently visible collaborator, after taking advice from those in the know that the hospital director would have no patience with a conversation conducted on chalkboards.

"These people are dying," Rebecca replied. "They know there is no cure in sight. If they choose to volunteer to test this method in the hope of clarifying its effects, why not allow them to?"

"You want to offer them hope, while shortening their lives?" Dr Harvey replied. "When the justification is...barely coherent."

"I can vouch for the observations on the bandage residues," Mrs Bambridge volunteered. "All my colleagues have cross-checked the results and the predictions. That level of agreement could hardly arise by chance; we can argue about the interpretation of the formulas, but they must be saying something about the underlying disease."

"They're saying that it exhibits a cyclic character that's related to the interaction calendar," Dr Harvey agreed. "But is that surprising? That's what life does: it follows those cycles. It doesn't validate every wild claim you choose to attach to the same facts."

Rebecca was beginning to look desperate. "If we find a cure, it won't just benefit the sufferers themselves," she said. "We're in a war over the etiology of this disease. Does that not tip the balance?"

Dr Harvey did not take this suggestion well. "The conflict with Myton has been used to justify all manner of extreme behavior, on both sides. I will not have it used to justify the abuse of my patients. Come back to me when you have some real evidence for your theories."

The delegation left the office and trudged dejectedly through the dust of the town square.

DISPERSION

"Your friend's made no progress with his calculations?" Mrs Bambridge asked.

"No," Alice replied. "He agrees that there should be an optimal time for the treatment, but he can't see a way to derive it from the mathematics alone."

Rebecca said, "We need a new round of experiments. Something that will subject the theory to a more stringent test. I'm sure we can think of—"

Alice heard a strange sound from behind her, high-pitched but too brief to properly characterize, and she turned in search of the source. People began shouting and the crowd shifted, pressing back toward her as if retreating from some threat, but in doing so blocking her view.

"What's happening?" Rebecca demanded irritably.

"Fetch a doctor!" someone screamed.

Alice tried to draw her mother out of the crush of bodies, but they seemed to be caught between one wave fleeing danger and a counterflow of spectators eager to discover what was going on. She wrapped an arm around Rebecca's shoulders and clung to her tightly, afraid someone would knock her to the ground and she'd be trampled in the rush.

The sound came again, then a man's voice bellowed in pain. "There's an archer on the roof!" someone shouted. Alice looked up, peering through the dust, and scanned the rooftops. She couldn't see a disembodied bow or quiver anywhere, but maybe the archer was laying them flat on the tiles between draws. The dust was too thin at that height to reveal an intruder, but anyone up there would have an easy time spotting their targets down in the square. Alice was sure that the risk of precisely this scenario had been pointed out to the chalk-clapping enthusiasts when they'd first started their campaign, but they'd refused to be dissuaded. Everyone knew that their own solution to the town's problems was the best thing imaginable.

She gave up trying to flee, and just did her best to shield her mother from the sea of jostling elbows. "Make way for the doctor!" a voice pleaded, then the arrow-pierced man began screaming again.

"I think they're closing in on the culprit," Mrs Bambridge suggested, nodding toward the roof of the meeting hall. Half a dozen men and women had already ascended, and they were scrambling over the tiles, swinging stone truncheons at the air around them. One woman picked up an arrow and waved it triumphantly over her head, but the bow was still nowhere in sight. Maybe the archer had left a hundred arrows on a dozen rooftops; that was what Alice would have done. A hundred arrows, and as many bows as she could carry. The whole square was probably covered with weaponry of various kinds, serving as decoys to distract the searchers just as much as it was serving as an actual supply.

Rebecca was starting to gasp for breath. "Give us some space!" Alice pleaded. "My mother's not well!"

"A man's bleeding to death here," a woman in front of them retorted. "Have some sense of proportion!"

"Follow me," Mrs Bambridge told Alice. She turned toward the edge of the square and began forcing her way through the scrum, ignoring all protests and retribution. Alice led Rebecca into the wake, huddled against her, elbowing anyone who tried to take their place.

They emerged from the crowd into a slightly less populated alleyway, and Rebecca stood leaning against the wall, wheezing. Alice heard raucous cheering behind her, and looked back to see the spectacle that had elicited this response.

On the roof of the hall, a figure she could not perceive directly was struggling inside a net, the strands made of rope but studded with stones. The Rytherans who'd gone in pursuit of the archer were gathered around, taking turns to bludgeon whoever they'd trapped. Alice's skin turned icy; she couldn't conceive of any way that the captive could be innocent, but she still recoiled from the sight of this faceless man or woman being beaten to death. The archer's victims had been nothing but phantoms, hollow forms moving below them through the dust, and now they'd been reduced to the same kind of husk in the eyes of their tormentors. Every act of vengeance seemed just, in the aftermath of the attack that provoked it—but for all she knew the person whose bones her fellow citizens were merrily crushing had only been recruited to the cause because some Rytheran zealot had stabbed their child to death in the middle of Myton.

"When's it going to end?" she asked.

"I have no idea," Rebecca replied, still struggling for each breath. "But it won't start...to end until we have the cure."

23

Alice collected the latest set of bloodied bandages from the ward and took them back to her workroom. The process of preparing the slides was routine by now, but she forced herself to concentrate, lest she confuse the two kinds of sample and end up ruining the observations.

She'd just washed the gloves she wore for this work, but she must not have rinsed them well enough, as some residue of soap was leaving waxy streaks on the slide covers. She set everything aside and stripped off the gloves, prepared to hunt down a new pair and start again.

To what end, though? To Dr Harvey and his colleagues, shadows of their adversary spinning through twelve-dimensional space would always be quasi-mystical nonsense.

A thousand observations of dried blood and dead tissue on a microscope slide wouldn't change that.

Alice went to the storeroom. Perversely, the tools and instruments with the best chance of surviving the flood had been those that had fallen into disuse and been packed away.

Her mother had given up trying to infect mice with the Dispersion more than a year before, but they still had the hypodermic syringes they'd used to try to introduce the pathogenic agent into the animals' bodies. The disease wasn't even known to be particularly infectious between human hosts. But no one had actually tried very hard to make that happen.

Alice took a syringe back to her workroom. She cut a piece off one of the infected bandages and dropped it in a vial of water.

As she sat watching the reddish-brown stain diffuse out into the liquid around it, she felt as if she was observing her own actions from afar, with a kind of skeptical amusement. She could resolve with great sincerity to jump off a mountain and see if an updraft of air caught her and delivered her to safety; that didn't mean she really had the courage to do anything of the kind.

She inserted the needle into the vial and drew some of the liquid into the syringe. But where to deliver it? A vein seemed excessively rash; even with the purest water, she suspected she'd be at risk of poisoning her blood with some entirely different affliction.

"A muscle it is, then," she muttered. She took down her trousers and thrust the needle into the side of her leg, then squeezed the plunger of the syringe until she could no longer bear the pain.

She cursed for a while, as softly as she could; if she sounded as if she was in distress, Mr Grevell might come running.

She pulled her trousers back on, then lay on the floor on her good side, waiting for the swelling to subside. It was still possible that nothing would happen; even lovers had not been known to pass the disease on to each other. And if she was as lucky as the mice had been, she would not have to confess what she'd done to anyone.

24

"I need to show you something," Alice told her mother, as she cleared away the dinner plates. "But please promise me, first, that you won't react intemperately."

"I will react in accordance to the circumstances," Rebecca replied.

"I've been interviewing helpers," Alice said. "I think I've found someone to do the cooking and cleaning for you."

Rebecca scowled in disbelief. "Why would we need someone like that? And even if we did, how would we pay for it?" She thought for a moment. "Are you marrying Christopher? Has he put you up to this?"

"I'm not marrying anyone, for now, but thanks for your good wishes."

"Then what is this nonsense? Am I that much of a burden to you?"

Alice leaned over and kissed her on the forehead. "Never. But I might be one on you, if I stay."

She undressed as much as necessary to reveal the wound that had developed in her quadriceps. She'd packed the hole with a cotton swab, but it was already coming loose.

"What have you done?" Rebecca wailed. "You stupid girl!"

"Someone had to do it."

Rebecca had grown so agitated that Alice was afraid she was going to have some kind of fit, but then she seemed to compose herself. "It's not too late," she decided, with a look of steely resolve.

"Not too late for what?"

"To amputate the limb. If you injected the disease agent locally, it might not have spread."

"Fuck that." Alice pulled her trousers up. "I'm not losing my leg."

"I'm not letting you die."

"I'm not going to die," Alice replied scornfully. "You were happy to offer the treatment to all the other patients. You must have had faith in it—or was that all for show?"

Rebecca stared at her as if she'd lost her mind. "They had nothing to lose! I wasn't asking anyone to put themselves in that position!"

"Well I've put myself there, so stop fretting about it. No one's cutting my leg off, so you'd better start talking to the group about the appropriate measurement protocols."

Rebecca put her head in her hands and emitted a long keening sound.

Alice said, "Maybe I'm wrong, but if I am, what's left for any of us? Ten years of war with Myton? Surrendering our land and fleeing? If the treatment doesn't work, I'd rather be dead."

In fact, she had no such preference, but it sounded suitably defiant. She didn't know if it would give her mother any comfort, but it roused her own spirits.

Rebecca turned to her. "I'm not going to force you to have an amputation," she said. "You're a grown woman, it's your choice to make."

"Thank you."

"Then if you're sure this is what you want, we'd better start making the best of it."

25

The ward for the Dispersion patients was on the hospital's second floor, and it had come through the flood unscathed. Alice had been prepared to find herself with a new perspective on the familiar surroundings, but she hadn't anticipated ending up in Timothy's old bed.

"I warned you not to be careless!" Mrs Jasper told Alice, after the nurses had left her to settle in. "Sticking your hands elbow deep in all our muck wasn't such a bright idea, was it?"

"How wise you were," Alice replied. "Let it be a lesson to everyone."

Mrs Jasper started coughing, and Alice felt a pang of guilt for mocking her. But she wasn't going to let the whole town know how she'd joined this select group; if Dr Harvey found out, he was as likely as not to blame her mother for putting her up to it.

It was her father who brought her the first day's worth of special meals. He sat by the bed while she ate, struggling to keep a cheerful demeanor. "I'm not the best cook in Myton," he said. "So you'll have to excuse my poor efforts."

"No, it's delicious," Alice insisted, crunching on the salad vegetables between mouthfuls of cold baked potato. "I know it's a lot of work tending the garden by yourself."

"It's easier than getting food brought in from Haverfield."

"This is like a vindication of your old theory," she mused. "If the wrong fraction comes into the body in too advanced a form, it can bypass the usual safeguards and be put to use. That's what we're relying on."

"I suppose so," he agreed. But the thought that the cure might mimic his discredited model of the disease didn't seem to give him any pleasure.

Alice said, "When this all comes back to you in a less pleasant form, please don't take that as a comment on your culinary skills."

The next evening, she woke with her gut contorted and her flesh aching. She didn't need to look for a clock to know that the transition had begun. The three false meals had infiltrated every part of her body, and their departure brought more of a shock than the occasional mouthful of bad water or counterfeit lettuce that everyone endured.

She reached down in the dark and gripped the edge of the stone tray beneath her bed, and when she raised it slightly she was gratified to find that she could feel the weight of its new contents.

When she finally drifted back to sleep, she dreamed that she was in the ballroom, dancing with her father beneath one of the spotlights. As he released her hands and spun away into the darkness she noticed a bird sitting on her shoulder, confused and agitated, pecking at her flesh. She tried to wave it away; she knew it didn't want to be there. But however she contorted herself, she couldn't reach it. It just sat there, pecking and pecking.

In the morning, Mr Grevell came to collect the samples neither of them could see; it wasn't safe for her father to leave the warehouse in his present state.

"Anything special I should put on the menu for you?" Mr Grevell asked.

"Is there such a thing as a fruit pie in Ridgewood?"

"Apple, strawberry, peach, or pomegranate?"

"You have all of that on hand?"

"My brother owns an orchard," he explained. "He sends me fresh provisions twice a week."

"Bring one of each kind," she suggested. "Just in case the Dispersion turns out to like one flavor more than the others."

Alice had brought a dozen things to read, but she couldn't concentrate on any of them. Mrs Jasper's cough had changed into a shallow rasping that was even harder to ignore. Alice struck her own ribs with her fist to try to gauge any shift in the way her body responded to the blow. The hole in her leg was visible, but if the disease spread to her lungs it could arrive without warning.

In the evening, her mother came with the results.

"The samples showed nothing unusual," she said.

"Do we know what's usual for such material?" Alice wondered. "Someone else without the disease should be mimicking my diet, for the sake of comparison."

"You should have thought of that sooner."

Alice laughed. "Never mind. So we shift the dose back slightly, to another point in the interaction cycle."

Rebecca was not so confident about the strategy. "What if the best time to do this depends on the fraction in question?"

"The symmetry gives us a map. The interactions don't all last for the same amount of time, but Timothy's equations say that if a dose of Mytonian food, at a particular time, hasn't drawn out the pathogen, we've as good as ruled it out for Ridgewood at a certain other time in the corresponding cycle. We don't need to check every combination; that would be redundant."

"Except that none of this has really been tested, has it?"

"Well, no," Alice agreed. "But if Timothy's whole model of the fractions was mistaken, then none of this has any chance of working."

Alice did the calculations, and Christopher checked them, under duress. "I don't like this," he said. "Life or death hanging on these numbers."

"Do you feel that way when you're building a bridge?"

He shook his head. "You know it's not the same."

"Not yet, but if we keep working on it, it will be."

"The body's more complicated than any bridge."

"That's true," Alice conceded. "But the fractions are no messier than the motions of the planets. We can't tell if it will be overcast or clear, but we can still predict every high tide, and every eclipse."

"And what if the thing you're relying on is a sun-shower in the middle of an eclipse?"

Alice said, "There's always luck, isn't there?"

When Mr Grevell brought his pies, Alice gorged herself, finishing them all. Mrs Jasper eyed her disapprovingly, and struggled to wheeze out a suitable reprimand. "You'll be sick, my girl!"

Alice said, "Maybe."

But she didn't vomit up the feast; her body clung on to every morsel tightly until it had no choice but to let go. Lying on her bed thrashing and sweating, she could feel the glorious damage she was doing as all the nutrients she'd provided to rebuild her flesh lost their purchase and fell away. Her body sequestered the things she had no control over: the products of respiration; the water that her ancestors had had no ability to refine. But even the most unsophisticated creature could learn to eat within its fraction, just by suffering through the aftermath when it strayed.

All it took to cheat the elaborate systems that protected her bodily integrity was a little perseverance. Why should the bird pecking at her shoulder be any harder to deceive?

She waited for the verdict.

Her mother said, "Nothing."

"What if I stopped eating Rytheran food altogether?" Alice wondered. "Just false meals instead, every day, around the clock?"

"You'd be dead in a week."

"Are you sure?"

"Very sure," Rebecca replied. "It was a form of medieval torture. Some deranged monarchs used to kill all their enemies that way."

"Why am I only hearing about this now?" Alice felt cheated. "Don't they say that all medicines are poison, and all poisons medicine; it's just a question of dosage?"

Rebecca said, "I didn't think it would do much for your morale to know that you were tying yourself to the rack. What do you want Mrs Bambridge to bring you? Once you know when you want it delivered?"

"Soup," Alice decided. "Bread and soup, for the prisoner in the tower."

When her mother had left, Alice thumped her ribs. Her chest felt hollow, but her breathing was still fine.

Mrs Bambridge's soup was delicious, but Alice couldn't keep it down. Had her stomach grown wise to the deception?

"I'm so sorry," she told Mrs Bambridge. "But can you bring me something more like hospital food?"

"I'll do my best."

The new layer of subterfuge helped: Alice retained all of the bland, poisonous medicine right up to the transition. But when it left her, it was like a knife raking over her flesh from the inside. "I'll confess to anything," she whispered. "Treason. Plotting against the king."

Her mother said, "This is making you weak. The nurse told me that there's blood in your urine."

Alice was confused; she hadn't seen Rebecca come in.

"But what about the slides?"

"There's still nothing. I'm sorry."

"I have to calculate the time for the next dose." Alice groped around on the table for her notebook.

Rebecca took her hands. "Christopher will do that."

Alice stared at her. "Are you lying to me? Are you trying to chop my leg off?"

"No."

She looked around the ward. "Where's Mrs Jasper?"

"She died last night."

Alice pulled her hands free and drummed on her chest. "What's left? What's left of me?"

Rebecca held her by the shoulders. "Do you want me to stop this, and just give you normal food?"

"No!" Alice cringed into the bed; she didn't know what was happening to her, but she couldn't stop what they'd started. "We just need to get the timing right."

"Then you have to trust me."

"I do."

Alice closed her eyes and fell back into the darkness. The bird was still on her shoulder, pecking away, but Alice let it be, reaching into her torso instead and pulling out handfuls of sawdust that she scattered on the floor.

Someone woke her. "Eat this." The woman spooned food into her mouth, and massaged her throat until she swallowed it.

DISPERSION

"Who am I?" Alice asked, bewildered.

"You're my daughter. It's all right. You have a fever, but you're going to be all right."

Alice slept, then the woman woke her again to feed her. Another woman came and helped her use the bedpan. She slept and danced and woke and ate and shat and slept and danced.

In the ballroom, her partners kept changing. She didn't recognize any of their faces, but she knew they were not the same. As they danced together, they'd offer her sweets, popping them right into her mouth, but when she looked down she'd see them rolling out of the cave that had once been her stomach.

"Wake up," a voice pleaded. "Just try this. Alice? Please. Christopher says this is the only time left. If it's ever going to work, it will be now."

Alice opened her eyes and let the hands around her slide her up against the pillows. When a spoon pressed against her lips, she opened her mouth and let the contents fall onto her tongue. She was tired, but she forced herself to continue, mouthful after mouthful.

When she finally closed her eyes, Timothy took her hand.

"I never had a chance to say goodbye," he said, waltzing her around beneath the light that shone on just the two of them. He was skeletally thin, but he seemed happy.

"I'm sorry I gave you so much pain."

"Don't fret about it. It's over." He gestured at her stomach. Feathers were falling from the cavity and scattering on the floor around their feet.

Alice peered down at her shoulder. The bird that had been tormenting her was gone. She looked up and caught a glimpse of its pale form, soaring away into the darkness.